Wylding Hall

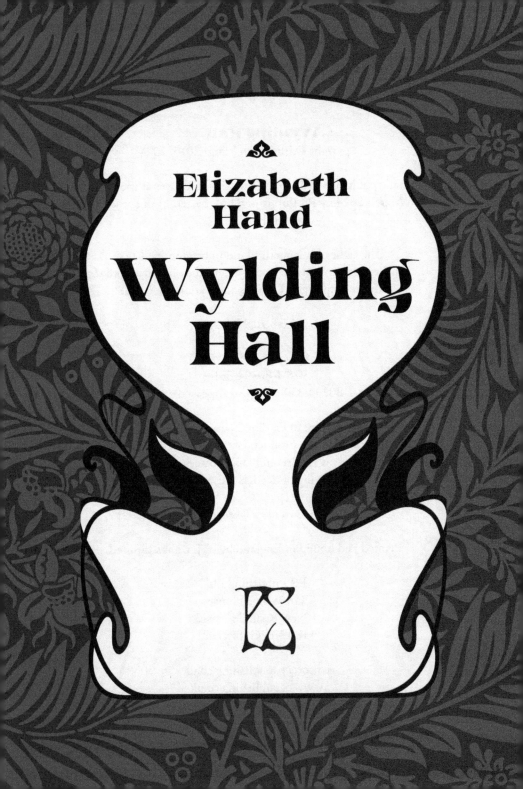

Elizabeth Hand

Wylding Hall

Wylding Hall

Originally published in 2015, this special hardcover edition is published in March 2024 by PS Publishing Ltd. by arrangement with the author.

The right of Elizabeth Hand to be identified as
the Author of this Work has been asserted by her in accordance
with the Copyright, Designs and Patents Act 1988.

2 4 6 8 10 9 7 5 3 1

ISBN
978-1-80394-331-2
978-1-80394-330-5 (signed slipcased edition)

Design & Layout by Christine M. Scott

Printed and bound in England by T. J. Books Limited

PS Publishing Ltd
Grosvenor House
1 New Road, Hornsea
HU18 1PG, England

editor@pspublishing.co.uk
www.pspublishing.co.uk

For Anne Wittman and Patrick Welsh

*With love and thanks for
helping me map the true Wylding Hall*

Introduction

For me, not all books are a pleasure to write. This one was. The title came to me sometime in the early Noughts, when I thought I might write a children's book, but that came to naught. The title then became attached to a contemporary YA novel set in an Adirondacks theater camp (don't ask) that I spent several painful years trying and failing to write. I finally (fortunately) gave up on that.

Sometime in 2014 I arrived in Camden Town, London, where I spend part of the year. The next day I was flying to Sweden, and I wandered to Camden Market, in search of something to read on the flight. In a bookstall I found a paperback copy of a Nick Drake bio for a quid. I'd read a couple of Drake bios but not this one, so I bought it and started reading it on the plane. I finished it on my return flight from Stockholm just a few days later.

Back in Camden Town I got sick. I recall lying in bed that night and much of the next day, feverish, when a story came to me — something to do with Nick Drake, the English countryside, Fairport Convention's time at Farley Chamberlayne, where they recorded their breakthrough album *Liege and Lief* after the tragic events that had occurred just a few months earlier. As too rarely happens, different voices started to dictate the story to me, and when I felt better, I began to write it down.

I'd recently read Rob Young's magisterial *Electric Eden: Unearthing Britain's Visionary Music*, and used it as a resource to fill in the many gaps in my knowledge of British folk music, in particular the roots of what became 1970s folk rock. (I ended up reading it three time.) I'd come of age listening to Fairport, Steeleye Span, Sandy Denny, Pentangle, The Incredible String Band, Tyrannosaurus Rex, John Renborne. By the early 1980s I'd discovered Nick Drake and Richard Thompson, whose work continues to haunt me. Over the following months, Wylding Hall gave me the opportunity to lose myself in the work of these artists, and many others, as I dove into the British folklore that's fascinated me since childhood. Cecil Sharp House is a five minute walk from where I live in Camden Town, and I spent many hours in their research library.

Writing this eccentric little story was a magical experience, and I was ecstatic when Pete Crowther (a fellow lover of folk music and lore) decided to take it on and publish it in 2015. It subsequently received the World Fantasy Award, and in the years since (almost ten!) I've been surprised and delighted to see it reach so many readers, many more than I ever could have imagined. I wrote it to honor the music and artists I love, and hope that others might share some of the joy I took in doing so.

With loving thanks to Pete and Nicky Crowther for their championing this book, and the songwriters that inspired it.

Elizabeth Hand
February, 2024

Wylding Hall

Thrice tosse these Oaken ashes in the ayre;
Thrice sit though mute in this inchained chayre:
And thrice three times tye up this true loves knot,
And murmur soft shee will, or shee will not.

Goe burn these poys'nous weedes in yon blew fire,
These Screeche-owles fethers, and this prickling bryier,
This Cypresse gathered at a dead mans grave;
That all thy feares and cares an end may have.

Then come you Fayries, dance with me a round,
Melt her hard heart with your melodious sound:
In vain are all the charmes I can devise,
She hath an Arte to breake them with her eyes.

— Thomas Campion, 1617

Dramatis Personae

Tom Haring: Producer, Moonthunder Records. Windhollow Faire's Manager

Windhollow Faire:

Lesley Stansall: Lead singer/songwriter
Ashton Moorehouse: Bassist
Jonathan Redheim: Drums, percussion
William Fogerty: Rhythm guitar, fiddle, mandolin
Julian Blake (deceased): Singer/songwriter, lead guitar

Patricia Kenyon: Journalist/Music critic
Nancy O'Neill: Professional psychic
Billy Thomas: Photographer, estate agent

Tom Haring, Manager/Producer

I was the one who found the house. A friend of my sister-in-law knew the owners; they were living in Barcelona that summer and the place was to let. Not cheaply, either, but I knew how badly everyone needed to get away, after the whole horrible situation with Arianna and this seemed as good a bolthole as any.

These days the new owners have had to put a fence up, to keep away the curious. Everyone knows what the place looks like because of the album cover, and now you can just Google the name and get directions down to the last millimetre.

But back then Wylding Hall was a mere dot on the ordnance survey map. You couldn't have found it with a compass. Most people go there now because of what happened while the band was living there and recording that second album. We have some ideas about what actually went on, of course, but the fans, they can only speculate. Which is always good for business.

Mostly it's the music, of course. Twenty years ago there was that millennium survey where *Wylding Hall* topped out at number seven, ahead of Oasis, which shocked everybody except for me. Then "Oaken Ashes" got used in that advert for, what was it? Some mobile company. So now there's the great Windhollow Faire backlash.

And inexplicable—even better, inexplicable *and* terrible—things are always good for the music business, right? Cynical but true.

Apart from when I drove out in the mobile unit and we laid down those rough tracks, I was only there a few times. You know, check in and see how the rehearsal process was going, make sure everyone's instruments were in one piece and they were getting their vitamins. And there's no point now in keeping anything off the record, right? We all knew what was going on down there, which in those days was mostly hash and acid.

And, of course everyone was so young. Julian was eighteen. So was Will. Ashton and Jon were what? Nineteen, maybe twenty. Lesley had just turned seventeen. I was the elder statesman at all of twenty-three.

Ah, those were golden days. You're going to say I'm tearing up here in front of the camera, aren't you? I don't give a fuck. They were golden boys and girls, that was a golden summer and we had the Summer King.

And we all know what happens to the Summer King. That girl from the album cover, she'd be the only one who knows what really went on. But we can't ask her, can we?

Will Fogerty, Rhythm Guitar; Fiddle; Mandolin

I knew Julian from school. We both grew up in Hampstead and attended the local comprehensive school. Posh boys compared to Ashton and Jon, which put us at a distinct disadvantage, I can tell you that! Ashton was part of the Muswell Hill music mafia, all those blokes knew each other—stand in the middle of Archway and throw a rock in any direction and you'd hit a folk musician.

Whereas if you threw a rock in Hampstead and hit anyone you'd end up in prison. There were days when I could have done with that happening to Ashton. He could be a right bastard.

Still, that was our hardship, mine and Julian's—not belonging to the working class. Me and Julian weren't at public school—what you Americans call private school—and Hampstead's North London, not posh Kensington. But Muswell Hill was where the best musicians came from. Something in the air. Or the drink, more likely.

I started on violin and Julian played the piano. I'm not sure when he took up the guitar. Once he did, it was as if he'd been born to it—he was an extraordinary guitar player. These crazy tunings would make it sound like he was playing a flute or a sitar, or a human voice. We used to play at the Hampstead Folk Club, which was a glorified name for an upper room above a pub. All the folk clubs were like that, up a stairway to a dark panelled room with chairs lined up and everyone smoking cigarettes and nursing their pint. If you were lucky, someone might have a joint and would pass it to you. Nothing heavier than that. No one paid to hear us sing, and none of us musicians got paid, unless you were someone like John Martyn.

But it was a good way to meet girls, I thought, so I dragged Julian along with me to take our turn at the front of the room. Girls loved it. Girls loved *him*, he could've played the kazoo and they'd be banging on his door. He was just too good-looking, but shy around the girls in those days. Even then, people wondered was he gay? If he was, I never saw any of it.

Lesley said she wondered sometimes, but I think—and this is off the record, Les and I are still close and I wouldn't want any hurt feelings; also, she has a temper—but I think Julian just wasn't attracted to her. Not that Les wasn't pretty. She was a lovely girl, we all fancied her. That's why we took her on!

But you know what I mean. She was a different type, physically, from Arianna. Lesley wasn't a waif, and even in school Jules always went for the wee girls with the big sad eyes. No stamina, girls like that. I would know, and Les was scary smart, which can be intimidating for a bloke, even someone as brilliant as Julian. Maybe more intimidating. I don't think he was accustomed to being with someone who was his equal. Musically, yes, but not someone who could match him intellectually. Especially a girl. And Lesley was American to boot, which in those days was a novelty, and also an affront to a lot of people. I mean, an American teenager singing traditional

English folk songs in a London pub? Some people came just to see her fail. Well, that didn't happen.

Lesley Stansall, Singer/Songwriter

He never talked about what happened with Arianna. The police report said she fell from a third floor window to the pavement. There were no bars across the window in Julian's flat, I do know that. She was depressive—that's what they'd say now, her and Julian both.

Suicide? How could it possibly matter all these years later, whether or not I think she killed herself?

She was a teenager, we were all teenagers. Today Arianna would be some gothy little girl hunched over her mobile. She was a beautiful child with a pretty voice. She didn't have it for the long haul.

Tom

Julian took Arianna's death very hard. He felt responsible—"I should have never let her into the flat that night, it was my fault we'd had an argument," etcetera, etcetera. They'd done a gig together at Middle Earth, just the two of them. Afterward he told her the rest of the band wanted to head off in a different direction, musically. She'd thought that her and Julian singing together would be the start of something, Simon and Garfunkel sort of duo. Instead it was the end. He was trying to give her a gentle kiss-off, but I think it had the opposite effect.

Jon Redheim, Drums and Percussion

I saw it coming with Arianna. She was drop-dead gorgeous but she was, you know, high maintenance. A cross between Nico and what's-her-name, that French singer. Juliette Greco. Always wearing black, back before everyone and his grandmother was wearing black. She was a big mope, Arianna, and we were well rid of her. There, I said it.

Ashton Moorehouse, Bass

We slept together once after a gig. She cried afterwards, said she'd betrayed Julian. I told her Julian couldn't give a fuck. Which was true, but I probably shouldn't have said it. She was beautiful but too skinny for my taste. I like a girl with meat on her bones. Julian, he always went for the ones a good wind would blow away.

Lesley

I can still remember when Tom told us he'd booked Wylding Hall for the summer. Ashton and Jon weren't happy about it. Ashton especially, he was royally pissed off. They were afraid of what they'd miss here in London. Girls, mostly, for Ashton. Boys for Jon, though no one was supposed to know that. And there's Tom with his high-minded idea that all anyone needed was a month in the country to recover from Arianna's death.

Yeah, I know: I'm being a snark, cause I wasn't with Windhollow Faire from the very beginning and didn't really know her. So sue me.

And it's true, with or without Arianna, they were getting a lot of gigs. *Windhollow Faire* had just come out that Christmas—their first album—and sales were good. There was no music press like there is now, you didn't have *Pitchfork* or YouTube and all that stuff. *Rolling Stone* had only been around for a few years, and *Record Mirror* and *NME*. There was no way to really publicise your band except by playing, like, constantly. Which they did.

But to be brutally honest, even before Arianna died they were getting tapped out. I'd heard Windhollow play a few times, and while they were good—I believe that "promising" is the overused adjective—they were never going to be much more than that if they didn't do something drastic.

And I know Tom could see that they were starting to flag, inspiration-wise. Which is why he suggested that Julian and Will come hear me at the Troubadour one night. I was doing a couple of Dylan covers, some Velvet Underground—hardly anyone here had heard of them—along with the usual stuff from the Child Ballads song-book. I saved my own songs for last. I knew I had them as soon as I did "Fallen Sky".

Will

My God, that girl could sing! Les opened her mouth and Julian and me looked at each other and just started laughing. By the time she got to "Fallen Sky" we were practically climbing over the tables to ask her to join Windhollow.

Tom

In retrospect, we should have told Arianna immediately that we'd found a new female singer. I should have told her. It was my responsibility as manager. The fact that Lesley was American must have been a real slap in the face for Arianna. I've taken the blame from the outset. Still, Julian never forgave himself.

That was the real reason I signed that summer's lease on Wylding Hall—to get Julian away from his bedsit in Gospel Oak, which, let me tell you, was the most god-awful depressing flat that you can imagine. I would have flung myself out the window, too, if I'd spent more than a week there.

Never mind, strike that. I don't need any more crazed fans blaming me for what happened. All I can say is that, at the time, spending three months at a beautiful old wreck of a stately home in the English countryside seemed like a good idea.

Hindsight is twenty-twenty. Isn't that what you say in America? But I didn't have hindsight. When it came to Windhollow Faire, I was utterly blind.

Lesley

I rode down there with Julian. He had a rickety Morris Minor, there was barely room for me once he'd got his guitar and other gear into it. Everyone else went down in the van.

I'd heard Julian sing before, and of course I had the first Windhollow album. But we'd never properly met. Word on the street was, Julian Blake was the most beautiful guy anyone had ever set eyes on. Typically, I was going to be contrarian: I was determined to be unimpressed.

The truth is, I was very, very shy. I was only seventeen, remember. My mum and stepdad were American. They both died when I was fifteen, in a car accident. My biological father was from Yorkshire; he'd been married before he met my mother and already had a family. I was born here in London when he and my mum were still together, so I had dual citizenship. We used to come over for summer vacations. I got to be close with my older sister, so after the accident I came here to live with her in Rotherhithe.

I was a bad student, but I was a good singer. My dad was brilliant—he used to sing along with whatever was on the radio, but he also knew all these old English folk songs. I learned by listening to him, harmonising. I just memorised whatever I could.

It was tough, coming to live here with my sister. People thought I was stuck-up because I was American. It was hard to make friends—I got pushed around a few times, but when I'd take a swing at them I'd be the one that got into trouble.

Eventually I just stopped going to school, and I guess because of the whole American thing, no one followed up on me. Plus it was the early 1970s—there were kids squatting everywhere in London. I went out to Eel Pie Island and joined the commune there for a while. That's when I started performing.

Julian was only a year older than me—fourteen months, to be exact—and he was cripplingly, almost pathologically, shy. Much worse than I was. Which of course I didn't realise when I drove down with him to Wylding Hall. I thought *he* was stuck up! He was from Hampstead. I was this blonde hippy from Connecticut, even though I'd been in London for a year. I looked older than seventeen, so at first he thought I was putting him off for being younger than me.

I didn't know that till Will told me. The two of them had grown up together. Will was almost like Julian's interpreter—sometimes Julian was so shy he'd just stand there right next to you and stare straight up into the sky for a quarter of an hour without saying a word. "Cloud Prince", I wrote that about Julian. The boy with the sky in his eyes.

Jon

It's true. When he was young, Julian was almost unearthly, he was so handsome it was difficult for me at first to keep my eyes from him. Spooky beautiful. People thought he was gay, but he wasn't. I was the one who was gay, though I only came out after that summer at Wylding Hall.

Believe me, I would have known if I'd had a snowflake's chance in hell with Julian, and there was just no way. I know, darling—you're looking at me now thinking, No shit, Sherlock! But you wouldn't have said that back then. I was a bit of a looker myself in those days.

Oh, right, you've seen the documentaries and all that on You-Tube. Yes, I *was* wasted back there behind the drum kit. But kinda cute, right?

Julian was beautiful. Those high cheekbones and all that dark hair flopping around his face. His skin was so pale you wanted to write on it like paper. And he had those amazing hands; big, big hands with long, long fingers. I used to watch him play guitar and just be hypnotised. He'd open his mouth and sing "Lost Tuesdays" or "Windhover Morn", and I'd just be a puddle—really! Me! The drummer! I used to watch him and just dream—*pray*—not that he'd kiss me, but that he'd write a song about me.

But you know, it was like he could barely stand to be touched—he'd almost flinch if you came too close to him. Not just me—I was used to guys not wanting to be too close to other blokes—but everyone. I'm sure that's what happened with Arianna; she thought they were in a relationship and here he could barely stand to touch her. That's why it was so strange about the girl.

If she had a name I never knew it. She was the only girl—the only person—I ever saw Julian with, physically. Not that I was perving on them, that's not what I mean; just that she was the only human creature I ever saw him willingly touch, or kiss. If in fact that's what she was.

Ashton

It was me, Will and Jonno in the van. We arrived around noon. I was driving—I was the only one had a license, besides Julian. What a bunch of fucking slackers. You take the A31 to Farnham, then it's pretty much nothing but winding lanes and little villages. Used to be, anyway. Heart of Hampshire, *Wind in the Willows* landscapes. One of the most beautiful places I've ever been. Probably all developed and paved over now; I've never had the heart to go back.

No? Well, that's a mercy. But I still won't be back.

I can still remember the first glimpse I had of Wylding Hall. There was no signpost, only a great boulder with the name carved on it, must have been five hundred years ago. Absolutely ancient.

The road between the hedgerows was so narrow that the branches poked in the windows on both sides, like they wanted to grab us. One scratched my cheek so badly it left a scar—see there? Fucking oak tree did that! It got infected, too.

So we drove and drove, and drove and drove and drove, and finally the hedgerows dropped back so we could see where the woods had been cleared a bit and you could see into the distance. Pastures, ancient field systems marked by stone walls, a thousand years old some of them, maybe older. There was a prehistoric barrow there as well, though we didn't know it at that point. I'm not superstitious, but Will is. He's the one spends all his time at Cecil Sharp House, digging through the archives for old murder ballads—"The Hangman's Kiss Upon My Cold Eyes", he found that one. If he'd known there was a barrow a stone's pitch from where we'd be sleeping, he would have stayed in Crouch End. What a fucking nutter. He's the one started all those rumours.

Look, I love Will—I'll kill anyone raises an eyebrow at him. But he's taken every pill and smoked every spliff and drunk every pint ever laid in front of him. He's done none of us any favours with his crazy theories. Same with Jonno. You can print that just as I spoke it.

Then what do *I* think happened? I don't have a fucking clue, but I'm not afraid to say I don't understand everything there is to know in this world.

She was the most beautiful young girl I've ever seen. I'll say that, too. I've been married five times and every one of them was a beautiful woman. But there was no one you ever saw looked like her. Looking at her made you want to claw your heart out, it ached so much. We all thought so, except for Les. I think she wanted to tear out the girl's heart instead.

Tom

Wylding Hall was remote, but that was part of its charm. For me, anyway—I wanted them as far from London as possible. Even now you can't get a mobile signal out there. I don't know how the new owners manage. Maybe they like it that way.

No distractions—that's what I wanted for the band. They needed to recover from Arianna's death. They were all traumatised to some degree, and Jon had just lost his mother to cancer. Just kids—they were all just kids, remember, especially Les. She'd been orphaned a few years earlier, lived with her alcoholic sister and her kids in some council flat in the East End before taking off to sleep rough on the streets. She's a tough old soul, Lesley. Even then, as a girl, you could see it. She was tough as a nut.

Anyway, that was my cunning plan: to spirit them all away to remotest Hampshire, have them live together in a sort of musical commune and see what happened. I mean, people do that, right? To young people, and we were all young, it seems like the most wonderful thing in the world, off on your own, remaking the world if you will. Sort of a utopian ideal. Hey, it was the Seventies.

And it did bear fruit, in that album, even if it took years for people to catch on. Progressive folk music was having its day in the sun, and Windhollow's first album fit that model. But *Wylding Hall* changed the game for that kind of music, and everything that came after as well. I'm very proud of it, and I know the others are, too. Brilliant work, not a duff song in there.

Not that Windhollow's first album was shabby. A few twee songs, like "Miss Marnie I Miss You" and "Another Fool in the Dark"—they hadn't gotten their stride, and Will was still going for those fiddle-dee-dee arrangements; I hadn't pounded that out of him yet.

The band's name, of course, I thought that was hopelessly twee. Windhollow Faire. Turns out that's where Ashton pulled his first girl, someplace in Oxfordshire. I've always wondered if she ever made the connection. Whoever she was.

But that second album—it was all a sort of amazing chemistry. Alchemy, Julian called it. He was into all that kind of thing—magick with a K, astrology, God knows what else. Palmistry, reading the bumps on your head. Casting spells. He wanted the album itself to be a kind of spell. An enchantment. You'd listen to it and without knowing it, you'd be changed. "Ensorcelled." That's his word, not mine! Back then, Julian believed in that kind of thing.

But you know, given the influence and power that album's had over the years, I can almost believe it, especially when you con-sider the shit storm of bad luck when it was first released.

Will

The house was a glorious wreck. Like some drunken grande dame who's lost everything except the clothes and jewels she's wearing and refuses to leave the after-party. I've known a few of those girls.

It wasn't immense. It wasn't Hogwarts or Manderley or Downton Abbey. But it was big and sprawling, and it was ancient. The oldest parts were pre-Norman—by "parts" I mean a few ruined brick walls out by the garden. Julian said there'd been an ancient Bronze Age settlement on the grounds, and he would know—that was Julian's thing, arcane knowledge. A lot of it was total bollocks, crystal pendulums and incense and tarot cards, all that crap he was into back then.

Ashton gives me such a goddamned hard time—he thinks I'm superstitious. And okay, yes, I'll knock wood, and I won't name the Scottish play in a theatre. But mostly I'm just respectful of old ways. I believe things for a reason, and in the old days they *did* things for a reason. And if you don't understand why—well, you might end up opening a few doors better left closed. That's all.

Julian never met a door he didn't try to open. He was quite knowledgeable about prehistory, studied at Cambridge for two terms. A very bright lad, you can understand why everyone makes such a fuss about his surname. I don't know if he'd researched Wylding Hall and that part of Hampshire before we arrived, or if he found some old book in the library, or what.

But he was the one who knew its history. From the moment we arrived, he seemed to know his way around the house.

"This is the Tudor Wing, this part's Norman, this was added after the Civil War, this is the crap Victorian addition." He just swanned in and began showing us around like he'd grown up there.

It was very odd, I have to say. I even asked him, have you been here before? He just shook his head and said no. He could just tell, he said.

That's why it's so strange that he didn't know about the barrow—the superstitions and whatnot. I don't know how he found it, if it was on the ordnance survey or he simply came upon it during one of his jaunts in the wood. The rest of us never knew it existed—we scarcely left the house some days, practicing. But Julian was always wandering off in the middle of the night or before the rest of us woke. He was always an early riser, when we were boys he'd be up before dawn.

"The best part of the day," he'd say. "Before it's had a chance to get broken." But everything gets broken eventually.

Tom

The oldest extant parts of the house were Tudor. An entire small Elizabethan-era manor tucked off to the back, surrounded by yew trees. Very lovely but dark—the trees were hundreds and hundreds of years old and overshadowed everything. A thousand years, maybe. Do trees live to be that old? You reached that part of the house by a narrow passage, very dim, with oak panelling. There was a long narrow hall with a minstrel's gallery, stone flags on the floor. On the upper floors there were any number of rooms. I couldn't tell you how many, because I only had a very cursory look when the estate agent showed me around. But what I saw was marvellous. Lovely carved panelling, small leaded windows. Beautiful National Heritage stuff. But very dark—not a lot of windows, and most of them deeply set into the walls.

Nobody slept in the oldest part of the house, though Les says she thinks that's where Julian and the girl went that first night, before going to his room. And Les was kind of stalking them, so she'd know. I suspect they wanted privacy, off on their own where no one could hear them.

Julian—so well mannered, quite gallant. Old-fashioned. I'm sure he thought he was doing the others a favour, quietly disappearing into the shadows with his lady-love. But it had the opposite effect, as such things do, especially when you're young and living in close quarters. It made everyone suspicious; a real daisy chain, everyone in love with the wrong person! The only ones who got what they wanted were Julian and the girl. I can't think of a single commune from those days that survived. All those utopias, undone by sexual rivalry and who didn't do the washing up!

So no, everyone pretty much stayed in the main part of Wylding Hall, which was more like a farmhouse and quite lovely; slate floors, a high-ceilinged whitewashed central hall with the original oak beams and fireplace, windows that looked out across the overgrown lawns to the Downs and woods beyond. That became the rehearsal room. They'd all meet there whenever they woke and stay there all night, sometimes, playing. Electricity had been brought in after the war. It hadn't been updated and was a bit dicey, but it did for the amps and guitars. Down the hall was an enormous old kitchen with an ancient gas cooker, a long trestle table, and mismatched chairs. There was a gas refrigerator that wobbled whenever you opened it. I'd checked everything out before I rented it, to make sure it worked. Which it did, barely.

There was a toilet room and a bath downstairs, and upstairs a number of bedrooms—seven, I think, in that wing. The furnishings were rather sparse but everyone had a bed. Some of the rooms had a desk, some had a wardrobe or chest of drawers. One had a great huge chair that was almost a throne—Jonno took that one. Julian's room had a proper desk facing a window with a beautiful view of the Downs to the west.

That's where he wrote "Windhover Morn"—you can see the photograph on the gatefold sleeve of his desk, with his notebook and that mess of music sheets and pens and pencils and his guitar on the bed. Such a beautiful view that was.

Ashton

My favourite part of the house was definitely the rehearsal room. That's where everything came down. We'd wander in by ones and twos, everyone was usually up before noon. Then we'd jam or listen to whatever song Les or Julian had been working on. Some days we'd get so caught up in playing that we'd forget to eat. Didn't forget to drink, especially Will. We had all our equipment set up in there, little PA system and all our guitars. Will's mandolin and sitar and God knows what. He even taught himself to play the viole de gambe, a true sign of a man with too much time on his hands. There was also Jonno's drum kit, and a beat-up old upright piano pushed into a corner. First thing we did was drag that out into the room. Julian used to play "Greensleeves" and John Dowland on it, songs that weren't composed for piano, but Julian played beautifully.

And you know, that piano was tuned perfectly. From the very beginning, I thought that was weird. Had someone come in to tune it? That would have been extremely odd, considering that absolutely nothing else had been done to the house to keep it up.

There were other weird things, too. Like the house always smelled of wood smoke—fresh wood smoke, like someone had a fire going in it somewhere. We'd been warned against doing that as the chimneys hadn't been cleaned in decades. At any rate, it was summer and far too warm for a fire. We'd open windows, burn joss sticks—no matter what we did, it still smelled of wood smoke. The rehearsal room less so than the rest of the house.

Then there was the Bird Room. This was a little corner room in the back of the house, near the old wing, not much bigger than a closet, with an eyebrow window high up, facing west. I was looking for a loo early one morning, just a few days after we arrived. Will always took forever in the loo and I got tired of waiting. I think that's where he taught himself to play the fucking viole.

None of us had really explored the place yet, so I wandered down this back corridor in my stockinged feet, trying doors to see if I could find a toilet. The knobs were hard to turn, and a few were locked, so I never did see what was inside. But most opened onto empty rooms, or rooms filled with old furniture mashed up against the walls or just piled on top of each other. Carven tables, chairs, wardrobes, settles—it was like *Antiques Roadshow* gone mad. Finally I reached the end of the hall and there was just one door left that I hadn't tried.

It opened right up. I barely touched the knob, but it turned like it was greased. I stepped in and immediately covered my mouth with my sleeve. The air smelled bad—truly foul. Not like a dead mouse or rat, not really like anything dead at all. Not like a clogged drain, either. It wasn't like anything I've ever encountered. It smelled *thick*, like I was breathing in some kind of vapour; marsh gas or something like that, though I've spent time in the Fens and I've never smelled something like that, not even close.

For a moment I thought I'd be sick, but I fought it off. I was wearing a bandanna—I had long hair then—so I covered my face with that. The room wasn't empty, but I couldn't clearly see what was there, just dark things sort of heaped on the floor. Rolled-up carpets, I thought—there were old oriental carpets everywhere. There was only a single small window high up in the far wall, all covered with dust and cobwebs, and it took a moment for my eyes to adjust.

It wasn't rolled-up carpets on the floor. It was birds, hundreds of birds, maybe thousands. I yelped and jumped backwards and bashed myself against the door. But the birds didn't move.

They were all dead. Little birds, wrens or sparrows—I didn't know birds. These were tiny, small enough to fit in your hand, and brown, with twisted tiny black claws, all piled atop each other like they'd been shovelled there. Some of them—a lot of them—were missing their beaks.

Have you ever seen a bird without its beak? Horrible, just tiny dead eyes and a hole in its face.

I whirled around to get back into the hall and something stabbed my foot. I thought I'd stepped on a nail, it hurt like hell but I didn't stop. I slammed the door behind me and hobbled fast as I could to the main hall. Will had finally gotten out of the loo by then so I went inside and locked the door. Last thing I wanted was for Will to see how worked up I was. I never told him, or anyone else.

My foot was bleeding hard, but when I pulled off my sock it wasn't a nail stuck there but a bird's beak, black and no bigger than a thorn. It must've taken me five minutes to work it out of my foot. How the hell it could have gotten in so deep? It had slid right through my sock. I staunched the cut best I could, tore up a wash towel and cleaned it and still it bled. I still have a scar there. See?

Lesley

My room was next to Julian's. It was a lovely room. I had a beautiful four-poster bed, and Tom had bought some very nice bed linens for me at Portobello Road, beautiful old French linen sheets and a pillowcase. There was also a big wardrobe and a *very* large mirror; because I was the girl, I suppose.

I loved it—it was by far the best room I'd ever lived in. Still is, probably. I'd sit in that big bed and write songs all day long. When we weren't playing together, I mean. I was reading a lot of poetry— John Clare, Rimbaud and Verlaine. Dylan and Leonard Cohen and Joni Mitchell. There weren't a lot of women songwriters then.

I was determined to change that.

The boys were down the hall, Will and Ashton and Jonno—Jonno I remember had the most ridiculous throne in his bedroom, he'd just lounge in it and listen to the same King Crimson record over and over again on his stereo. For, like, *three hours* at a stretch. Then he'd come down and grab something to eat and we'd all play together in the big room.

Jon

It's true. I think I was stoned twenty out of twenty four hours back then. Me and Will. Ashton was more of a boozer, him and Les would go off to the pub some days. They were the only ones got to know the locals.

Will

No, I don't drink anymore. I've been sober for thirty-seven years now, longer than you've been alive. Back then, I could pack it away. Occupational hazard of the folksinger in those days. Rock and rollers, too. Les, she still does—you can see that on her face. Don't print that. She has her reasons.

A typical day? Hmm, hard to say. I'm not sure if a typical day would start with the day or with the night. Night, probably.

All right: for the purposes of the documentary I'll say day. Julian would be up at daybreak no matter how little sleep he'd got, but the rest of us rose a bit later, say nine or ten. That sounds early to you? Well, youngster, it felt that way to me, too!

But there was a feeling we all had, that we were in a magic place, and we wanted to make the most of it. And we were young, so our powers of recovery were remarkable. We could drink all night, smoke till the house was spinning, do the odd bit of windowpane or blotter, busk at the pub if we needed a bit of ready cash for groceries, and still pop up bright-eyed, bushy-tailed and hop down to the living room, strap on our mighty axes and get to work.

Still—"typical day"?

I don't think those were typical days. Truly. They were halcyon days.

What does that mean? It's from a myth told by Ovid. Alcyone is the original name—the daughter of the wind god. Her lover Ceyx was a king and the son of the morning star. Against Alcyone's wishes, he set sail on a long journey across the sea. A terrible storm rose up and he was drowned, along with everyone on board his ship. Weeks later, Alcyone discovered his body washed up on shore, and her grief was so great she drowned herself.

But the gods took pity on her—on both of them—and turned them into birds. Kingfishers. So every summer there's six or seven days of perfect calm, perfect sun. They call those halcyon days, in memory of Alcyone.

That's how we lived at Wylding Hall, kingfisher days and golden nights. There was an enchantment on us, you can hear it in the music on the record. But the magic on that record is only a shadow of what we experienced then, playing together.

Yeah, okay, "shadow" doesn't really work, does it? Mixing metaphors.

An echo—that's what you hear on the album. An echo of what we created when we were all in that room together, Julian and Les, Ashton and me, mad Jon bashing away at his drum kit, with the sun in those great windows like they were gold not glass. We'd play for hours, until Julian broke a string or Tom rang on the phone. We'd all take a break for a slash or a smoke; and back to it.

You don't know what it's like, making music like that—I didn't, I couldn't have imagined it, until Wylding Hall. Julian was writing these songs, every morning he'd come up with something new, or a new version of one he'd just written. He'd grab his guitar and start picking out the melody and begin to sing in that whispery voice. After a minute Les would pick it up and join in. I'd follow them, and Ashton, and Jonno would suddenly erupt on the drums. And we'd just...play.

I've never known anything like it. Music, it's always hard to describe, isn't it? You can describe what it's like to *hear* a song, how it makes you feel, what you were doing when you first heard it. You can describe what it's like to write it, technically, and how to play it—the chord changes, slow down here, pick it up here. A Minor 7, C Major.

But this—this was different. It's a cliché to say something's like a shared dream, like a movie or a concert—you know, "We got wasted and stayed till the lights went up and then we stumbled home and it was all like a dream."

This wasn't like a dream. It was like being lost; not in the dark but in the light. Blinding sun through the windows and that fug of smoke from cigs and spliffs, motes in the air like something alive, atoms or insects all silver in the smoke. You couldn't see to find your way, we couldn't even see each other's faces, it was so bright and so much smoke. You could only hear the music and so you followed that. Lesley's deep voice and Julian's sweet one, Jon grabbing the edge of his cymbal so you could only hear this thin silvery sound.

Ashton's bass. Me and that mandolin I built from a kit; Les wailing until she nearly passed out. Julian's guitar. You couldn't see him at all—he stood at the very back where it was dark, furthest from the window. I swear I can still hear him.

There was a song by Davey Graham, "Anji", very famous guitar tune, very difficult to play. Every kid who picked up a guitar would try to master it and let me tell you, it was hell to play. No YouTube videos or guitar school to teach you, no Jimmy Page master class.

But Julian figured it out back when we were still at school. I remember I was amazed but also so jealous, I was just about sick.

I swear to God, he played it better than Graham did. Better than anyone. He tuned that Gibson to some scale only he could hear; you couldn't mistake it for anything else. The rest of us just followed it, like a thread through the maze.

I always thought the rehearsal room was the one space that didn't feel like it had a history attached to it. There wasn't the bizarre sense that we were intruding there, like I got in other parts of Wylding Hall. Whatever history that room had, it was *our* history. We laid it down, made our mark upon the place. Sometimes I feel like we might still be there, all of us playing together, if it hadn't been for what happened.

Lesley

Julian gave me a book to read that summer. It was when we first got involved, a week or so after we arrived at Wylding Hall. He could be so shy. He didn't much like to be touched. The first time he kissed me, I thought I might pass out. Or he would.

But when it came to things he was really interested in he was like a kid, he'd get so excited; in a quiet way—he never raised his voice, but he'd laugh. He'd sound almost delirious when he laughed, it was like it was some huge release for him, like orgasm or a sneeze. He'd get breathless.

We were in his room, in bed—the first time we slept together. It was wonderful. Early morning, the sun just coming in the window—that lovely window he had, you could see for miles on end, over the forest and Downs to where the hills turned lavender; they were so far off.

But at the same time you could see a church spire in the village and the roof of the pub, and this ruined tower that we were never able to find, though it was quite close by, in a copse not far from the barrow, though we hadn't found that yet, either. It was like looking into the wrong end of a telescope and the right end, both at the same time. It was a very strange window.

We were lying in bed, and I was thinking I might get up to take a leak and see about something to eat. I started to get out of bed when Julian stopped me.

"Hold on," he said, and leaned over the side. It was a high four-poster bed like mine, you could have hidden another person under it. He kept all kinds of things there, books mostly and records; not the ones he was playing, the ones he was looking at. Album art back then was so fantastic. You'd get stoned, put on a record then listen to it endlessly while you stared at the album cover.

Ah, the things you're forced to do without wifi.

He had stacks and stacks of books under there. Carlos Castaneda, Paul Bowles. A deck of tarot cards. He'd discovered Wylding Hall's library, tucked away in the oldest part of the house. I hadn't ventured there yet.

But Julian had. That's how we got together. He was sitting outside beneath one of those massive oak trees, reading some massive book. I pretended to grab at it and he got very stroppy so I apologised immediately. I was still getting to know all of them—I was still very much the new girl. Very conscious of being wrong footed.

Julian couldn't have been sweeter, though, said he hadn't meant to lash out at me, just it was a very old book he'd found, something from the old Tudor library and he wasn't even sure we were meant to go in there. Apparently he'd found the library the second day, on one of his pre-dawn rambles, and had been taking some of the books back to his bedroom to read.

He was impressed when I told him I'd been reading Rimbaud and John Clare. You don't know Clare? The mad poet who slept in hedgerows?

And little wren that many a time hath sought
Shelter from showers in huts where I did dwell
Tenting my sheep and still they come to tell
The happy stories of the past again.

I could quote him from memory. I think that's when Julian decided he'd take me seriously.

He had some ancient-looking volumes under his bed. Leather-bound. Some of them were quite small, the size of your hand. I remember feeling excited, thinking he was going to show me some weird esoteric thing he'd discovered, like an incunabula or something like that.

But it was just a paperback by Mircea Eliade, *The Sacred and the Profane.*

"Do you know this?" He held it in those big hands as though it were a butterfly he'd caught. "It's brilliant. There's two kinds of time, he says—sacred time and profane time. The outside, everyday world—you know, where you go to work, go to school, that sort of thing—that's profane time.

"But things like Christmas or holidays, any kind of religious ritual or shared experience, like performing together, or a play—those take place in sacred time. It's like this—"

He grabbed a pen and drew on the inside cover of the paperback. A little Venn diagram, two intersecting circles.

"—A circle within a circle. Do you see? This big circle is profane time. This one's sacred time. The two co-exist, but we only step into sacred time when we intentionally make space for it—like at Christmas, or the Jewish High Holy Days—or if something extraordinary happens. You know that feeling you get, that time is passing faster or slower? Well, it really is moving differently. When you step into sacred time, you're actually moving sideways, into a different space that's inside the normal world. It's folded in. Do you see?"

I stared at him and shook my head. "No," I said, then sniffed at his hair. "You been smoking already, Julian?"

He frowned. He didn't like it when you got on him about drugs. "Not yet. All right, what about this..."

He scrabbled at his desk for a blank sheet of paper, and I just watched him. You've seen the photos, so you know how beautiful he was when he was young. But really, they barely captured him. He stooped so much of the time, you never saw how tall he actually was.

He wasn't a sylph—he was big-boned, long lanky arms and legs and that marvellous hair; thick and straight and glossy, it felt like honey pouring through your fingers. He always wore the same brown corduroy jacket, a little short in the arms so you could see his wrists and his wristwatch, an old-fashioned one that you had to wind every day. It was expensive, I think he'd received it when he graduated from secondary school. Lots of fancy dials and second hands—is there something smaller than a second? If there is, Julian's watch had a hand that measured that. He was always checking it, and I was always checking *him*. I could have stared at him all day. I *did* stare at him all day, sometimes, when we were rehearsing.

Eventually he found a piece of white paper, drew something on it and folded it, like a fan.

"Now look at this." He held it up: a narrow, folded rectangle of blank paper. "This is us, now. Profane time."

I felt a bit of a stab at that, because we'd just spent the night together, and for me, that had been sacred time. But I only nodded.

"Okay then. Taa daa—" He unfolded the paper so I could see what he'd drawn—a simple landscape, hills and trees, sun coming up on the horizon. "Here's what's inside—a whole other world! Well, it's a bit bigger than this," he added, and laughed. "But that's what it's like…"

For the next few minutes he sat, and slowly folded and unfolded the paper, staring at it intently; almost as though he were meditating, or seeing something there that I couldn't. At the time I thought he probably was just stoned; grabbed a few hits while I was in the loo. Now I'm not so sure.

Ashton

The village pub was called The Wren. It's still there, I think; Windhollow's fans have given it good business over the years. Tom gave us a group allowance for food, most of which went on booze. Jon was always trying out some special way of eating, horrible miso soup and brown rice. Just about made me puke every time I saw him digging into it. The rest of us survived on bacon and eggs, maybe the occasional lamb stew. It was all very *Withnail and I*, only without Uncle Monty. Only I wasn't up to drinking the paint thinner. Not yet, anyway.

There was a local farmer who we bought from; Silas Thomas, a wretched old man like a character from a Hardy novel. He was always warning us off wandering the Downs after dark or getting lost in the woods; warning Julian, mostly, as he was the only one who did things like that. Tom must've paid him off, Silas, as he brought food round a couple days a week. Milk and eggs and rashers, and brown bread he must have made himself. I don't think he had a wife. If he did I never saw her.

But sometimes, you know, the body needs something more. Different food, different faces. Les and I were the ones who first ventured down to the Wren. She was a good girl for holding her drink and I quite fancied her. Not as thin as she's gotten since the cancer.

In those days she cut a striking figure. Crazy blonde hair, and those big blue eyes. She dressed sharp, too—long skirts and dresses, lace-up boots and flowing scarves, all kinds of shiny bits and bobs. Hippy royalty, we were. Not like you wankers with your black hoodies and earbuds.

Probably Tom should have thought it out better. Four blokes and Les the only girl—you could see how that might become a troublesome equation. I was furious when I realised Les and Julian were doing more than practice up in their bedrooms—murderously jealous, but only for a few weeks. Once the girl came on the scene, that put an end to Les and Julian's great romance.

It was a Friday night when we first went down to The Wren, Les and me. We decided we were going to busk at the pub and make a bit of dosh. We were skint, all of us, and we'd run through whatever money Tom had left us. If Old Man Silas hadn't been coming by we would've starved. Tom was supposed to drive down for a weekend to fill our coffers but that hadn't happened yet. The whole point of us being at Wylding Hall was *not* to have visitors, even our manager.

And we didn't really want any. Odd as that sounds to you—really, can you imagine being totally cut off, no mobiles, no interwebs? We couldn't even use the phone except in emergencies—it cost the earth.

So did petrol. We'd filled the van's tank before we first arrived but it was half-empty by now, and we were very cautious about taking it anyplace. It was held together with bits of string and old tin cans and I was always terrified it would die and that would be it: we'd be stranded in darkest fucking Hampshire. As far as I know, Julian's car never moved the whole time we were there.

I know: to you lot it sounds like hell, but to us it was heavenly.

Still, even in heaven you want a change from boiled eggs and plonk. So one day I fired up the van and drove me and Les into town. Understand that I mean "town" only in the sense that there was a road running through it. A pub and half-a-dozen houses, chickens in the street.

But The Wren was a proper pub with a regular clientele. Les charmed the barman into giving us something to eat: ploughman's lunch. Big slabs of white bread and ham and good cheddar and pickles. And great ale; it was a free house so the ale was brewed only a few miles off. We drank a few rounds then stood the barman for a few, by which time he was ready to take Lesley straight to bed. His name was Reg, good old Reg. Died some years back. He was feeling quite jolly when Les asked if we could sing later in the evening.

"What, are you a nightingale? I thought you were a peacock!" He leaned across the bar to tug at her scarf; it was printed with peacock feathers, and she wore earrings made from them, too.

"Peacocks scream. This bird sings like an angel." I put my arm around her but Les pushed me away and turned back to Reg.

"I do," she said. "I sing like an angel. In London people pay a lot of money to hear me sing. But for you, Reg—*just you*—I will make an exception."

Then she grabbed him and kissed him on the cheek, and that was all it took. Neither of us had a guitar with us, and I certainly wasn't lugging around my bass, so we just...sang. That's how we used to do it at the basement of Trois Frères at those all-night gigs, when anyone could stand up in the room and sing three songs. That's if they could still stand. But Lesley had a hollow leg in those days and so did I. Drink is what kept us standing.

We sang "Cloud Prince" and "Unquiet Grave"; I remember because Will had just taught us "Unquiet Grave" during our first day at Wylding Hall. You know that one?

My lips they are as cold as clay, my breath smells earthy strong,
And if you kiss my cold lips your days won't be long,
Go fetch me water from the desert and blood from a stone,
Go fetch me milk from a maid's breast that man's never known.

The punters loved it. Reg shouted out to everyone that we were very special singers down from London and Lesley was the next Dusty Springfield. Some shite like that.

They loved it—loved her. For some of them she was the first American they'd ever seen, and that might have been the first time they'd seen anyone who looked like her, with those leather boots, wild blonde hair and peacock glory. What a sight she was! Pissed as a bloody newt, of course—she was purely slap happy when we finally finished singing. The lads shouted for another song, but she just laughed and said she'd be back with more of her friends.

"We don't want your friends!" some bloke yelled. "You're woman enough for all of us!"

We got seven quid that night. Hundred pounds that'd be worth now, almost a hundred and fifty dollars; enough for a few bottles of wine and some chocolate cake, sweets and bananas, whiskey and fags. Not bad for three songs.

Will

One of the songs they sang that night was "Unquiet Grave". I wasn't there but Ashton told me when they got home. I'd found it amongst the Child Ballads at Cecil Sharp House back in London. A very old ballad, very grim.

"Why'd you choose that one?" I asked him. I thought it was strange. Usually Ashton went for the jigs and dance songs, the old knees-up. He said he wanted to hear Lesley sing it in front of an audience.

I wouldn't have chosen that song. Not for a first time out, there in the country. It's a warning, that song; the way some old songs or nursery rhymes are ways of memorising recipes, or history, or directions to a place. "Unquiet Grave" is like that. It's a warning.

No, I don't blame Ashton for what happened. But I do think it was a bit of bad fortune, to choose that particular song.

I wish I'd gone with them to The Wren that first night. I was the only one in the band who actually knew something about folk music. Ashton and Jon, they had more of a rock and roll background. They had no trouble picking up the songs and the instrumentation, but until we went to Wylding Hall they'd never done anything in the way of research into old music. They'd just pick up whatever song was making the rounds and try to put a stamp on it.

Julian was different. He had a better idea than anyone, even me, as to exactly what those songs were about and what they meant. But I wasn't aware of that at the time.

And Les is American. Today, she knows just as much about folk songs as I do, but back then she picked it up because that's what you did—if you weren't going to be in a rock and roll band, you'd sing folk songs. Bob Dylan, Joan Baez, Judy Collins, they all did riffs on English folk. Lesley had the voice for it; more soulful than someone like Grace Slick, and she didn't sound like she was giving you a lecture, the way Joan Baez did.

Les had a magical voice. She was just starting to write her own songs, so she'd pretty much sing whatever you handed to her.

I would never have expected her to recognise the photos in The Wren, but I might have thought that Ashton would mention them. He knew how caught up I was with folklore and ritual. Then again, maybe that's why he *didn't* mention them. Or maybe he was just too pissed to notice them at all.

I went up to the pub by myself a few days later. I was in the mood for a walk, and sometimes it felt like such a pressure cooker at Wylding Hall. I could hear Julian and Lesley going at it in Julian's room. Les, mostly, as I never heard much out of Julian. He wasn't what you called hot-blooded, not until the girl showed up.

Still, him and Les were in the throes of an affair, even if it was mostly one-sided. Made me miss my girlfriend, Nancy. Jonno— well, I wasn't sure what Jonno got up to. He didn't tell the rest of us he was gay till that autumn. I'm pretty sure he told me some story about a girl back in Chelsea.

But I missed Nancy terribly. I spent a lot of time feeling sorry for myself in my room, playing mournful songs.

That particular day, I decided to really feel sorry for myself and tromped off to the pub. Took the better part of an hour to get there on foot, and I was thirsty when I arrived. Had a pint of good ale, sat off by myself. There were only a few geezers there, and they left me alone. Fine by me.

After a while I got a second pint, and was starting on a third when I decided to take a slash. Heading back from the bog I noticed several photos on the wall. Old photographs, black and white, cheap frames; the kind of thing you see in every pub in England—the local rugby team, or someone's brother with the goalie from Manchester United, or the great granddad of the proprietor.

But these were different. At first I thought they were very old, early 1900s, maybe even older, because of the subject matter. All that time I spent at Cecil Sharp House, poring through their archives and old books—well, I recognised these photos. Not the exact photos, but the subject matter.

They showed a group of boys in ragamuffin finery—old frock-coats too big for them, knee-high boots or soft leather shoes, top hats or workmen's caps stuck with sprigs of ivy and evergreen. It was wintertime, a few inches of snow on the ground. One of the photos showed the boys knocking at the door of a cottage. In another they stood all in a row, each of them holding what looked like a walking stick, staring at the camera with that strange grim look you see in old photos; like they'd been told "Whatever you do, *don't smile.*" In the last photograph they stood atop a little hill in a half-circle.

You're thinking, so what?

Well, here's the thing: in every photo, one boy held what looked like a cage, covered with more greenery. It wasn't a proper cage, though, but two hoops made of stripped willow branches, placed one inside the other, then strung with ivy and holly. Something was suspended from the spot where the two branches crossed at the top. I could barely make it out in the picture that showed them at the cottage door, but it showed more clearly in the other two.

In the first photo—the one taken on the hill—the cage was empty, and it sat at the feet of the smallest boy. In the second photo, where they stood all together with the trees behind them, the same boy had the willow cage, held out in front of him as though it were a lantern. This was more of a close-up, so I could see what was hung inside the willow round. A dead bird, strung up by one foot. Not a grouse or partridge or pheasant, something you might hunt to eat, but a tiny bird, so small that it wouldn't make more than a mouthful.

But they weren't going to eat it. I knew because I'd seen pictures of the same sort of thing at Cecil Sharp House. All the sport was in the hunting, and then the door-to-door in the village, displaying the dead bird and singing.

Away to the wood, says Dick to John,
Away to the woods, says every one!
And what do ye there, ye merry men?
We hunt to the death the wicked witch-wren.

It's an ancient carol, sung on the day after Christmas—Boxing Day, St. Stephen's Day. You don't celebrate it in the U.S.

But way back when those photos were taken, all the boys and men of a village would walk out armed with cudgels and harry the wrens out of the underbrush, then club them out of the air. Wrens don't fly very high.

Yes, I know, it sounds barbaric. It *is* barbaric. But this was the only time you were allowed to kill a wren—all sorts of terrible things happen if you kill it out of season. I think in some places it might even have been illegal.

Once upon a time, they did this all across the British Isles, in England and Ireland and Scotland and Wales. There are all kinds of songs about it—"The Cutty Wren", that's the one I just sang, and "Please to see the King". Christmas carols, but they're really quite ancient songs. You'd kill your wren then parade it around the village. It represented the old year sacrificed so that the new year could rise from his ashes.

That's how some of the songs go. Others say that the wren's a wicked creature, a fairy woman. You still see the wren on Christmas cards here in England, though everyone's forgotten what it represents. It's all a bit Wicker Man. And the name of the pub, that should have been a clue, right?

Well, I was terribly excited by this discovery. From what I'd read, the wren hunt had died out everywhere except the Isle of Man, and even there it's been turned into a tourist holiday, like the Padstow Hobby Horse.

Yet the photos in the pub were all dated 1947. Even if the ritual hadn't been performed a single time since then, it was the most recent survival of the wren hunt in England that I'd ever heard of.

I walked over to ask the barman what he knew about it. Not a thing, he said; he was from Canterbury and had only moved to the village after he married a local girl. He told me to ask some of the old timers.

You can imagine how that went down. They just took one look at me and turned away laughing or scowling. I knew better than to keep on at them, so I finished my pint and walked home. I mentioned the photos to Ashton and Les, but they hadn't noticed them. Next time I was at the pub, they were gone. Barman said the geezer who'd hung them there wanted them back.

Like I said, that should have made me think twice. But it didn't.

Tom

Ashton was worried I'd be ticked off about them singing down at the pub. To be honest, I was a bit annoyed. Windhollow wasn't so well-known then, nothing like now—can you imagine the scene today, if they'd suddenly shown up at your local and just started playing?

But people *did* know them, certainly in London they did, and there was probably the odd hippy living in a caravan somewhere in Hampshire who might have heard about it and invited his friends down.

I just didn't want them to be distracted. The songs that ended up on the *Wylding Hall* album were already starting to come together. I was afraid word would get out and there'd be a bunch of hippies crashed at Wylding Hall and that would be the end of it.

And yes, I was concerned about Julian; that he'd meet up with bad companions and smoke himself into oblivion. He was whip-smart but somewhat of a social and emotional innocent. You could see it pained him to talk to people he didn't know—he was a publicist's nightmare—and that acute shyness could come off as arrogance, especially in someone so good-looking.

Have you ever noticed how we accord special privileges, almost magical powers, to people who are beautiful? Particularly if they're beautiful and talented, like Julian. I have no idea what happened, him and that girl. I never met her, but that's what I mean by bad companions. Not to blame someone I never met—for all I know, she might have been as much of an innocent as Julian. Probably she was. I'm very curious as to what they'll find when they dig up that long barrow.

Jon

We only played the pub a few times that summer. When Tom found out he made a point of sending us more dosh, so we wouldn't be tempted to do it too often. I enjoyed it, but he was right—people were picking up on it, that we'd played at The Wren. God knows how they found out, there were no mobiles or internet. The village barely had a telephone service. I think you'd have been better off sending messages by carrier pigeon. Perhaps that's what they did.

Anyway, I'm sure that's why Tom decided to come down with the mobile unit—he didn't want to chance someone else showing up with a tape recorder during one of our gigs.

Of course, I wasn't dragging my drum kit down to the local, so whenever we played there I'd have nothing but a little tambour and bells. It felt almost medieval, which was lovely, really—it felt like we truly were wandering bards. Troubadours.

Well, maybe not me so much. I was always a bit of the outlier. I never set out to play any kind of folk or trad—I was a rocker who went astray; up there on Muswell Hill with the Davies brothers. That's who I wanted to be, not a bloody little folkie. I saw myself more as John Bonham. Or Long John Baldry.

But me and Ashton were mates from school, and he'd been picking up work for a few years before we started the band. A good bass player is worth his weight in gold, and Ashton was brilliant. You know how they called John Entwhistle the Ox? Ashton was the Oak, because of his name—the mighty Ash, the mighty Oak.

He was a tough nut, Ashton, always difficult to get along with. But the birds loved him—the young girls—and that meant he always had an audience. He'd played with Will at a few pick-up gigs in London. They decided to put a band together and they were looking for a drummer, so that was me. Ashton met Arianna at some pub where he'd been playing. Will brought Julian. Arianna was gorgeous, and so was Julian. Both very photogenic, looked great onstage and when we did *The Old Grey Whistle Test.*

But Arianna was out of her depth. Everyone saw that. When we cut our first album, *Windhollow Faire*, Jack Brace produced it and he did a fine job of covering up her weaknesses in the studio. But in order to survive, the band needed to play almost constantly, and Arianna simply wasn't up to it. She had a pretty voice, she could carry a tune—that was never a problem. But she had no depth. She couldn't interpret a song, place her stamp on it. Unlike Lesley, who fairly stomped on it!

And that's what you need in folk music. These are songs that have been around for hundreds, maybe thousands of years. They existed for centuries before any kind of recording was possible, even before people could write, for God's sake! So the only way those songs lived and got passed on was by singers. The better singer you were, the more likely it was people were going to turn out to hear you and remember you—and remember the song—whether it was at a pub or wedding or ceilidh, or just a knot of people seeking shelter under a tree during a storm.

It's a kind of time machine, really, the way you can trace a song from whoever's singing it now back through the years—Dylan or Johnny Cash, Joanna Newsom or Vashti Bunyan—on through all those nameless folk who kept it alive a thousand years ago. People talk about carrying the torch but I always think of that man they found in the ice up in the Alps. He'd been under the snow for 1200 years and when they discovered him he was still wearing his clothes, a cloak of woven grass and a bearskin cap, and in his pocket they found a little bag of grass and tinder and a bit of dead coal. That was the live spark he'd been carrying, the bright ember he kept in his pocket to start a fire whenever he stopped.

You'd have to be so careful, more care than we can even imagine, to keep that one spark alive. Because that's what kept you alive, in the cold and the dark.

Folk music is like that, and by folk I mean whatever music it is that you love, whatever music it is that sustains you. It's the spark that keeps us alive in the cold and night, the fire we all gather in front of so we know we're not alone in the dark. And the longer I live, the colder and darker it gets. A song like "Windhover Morn" can keep your heart beating when the doctors can't. You might laugh at that but it's true.

Nancy O'Neill

I was Will's girlfriend for two years, from before their first album to a year or so after *Wylding Hall*. I was an outsider—I wasn't from the folk scene, or any music scene at all. I was in art school at the Slade and saw an early show that Windhollow did there. It was in the cafeteria, not a proper stage or anything, and only about thirty people in the audience. But I was impressed, mostly by Will's looks. He was quite tasty; long curly red hair and a moustache. A big man. I made him get rid of the beard after we started dating.

Guys in the trad scene tended to wear flannel shirts and corduroys. I think the intent was that they should look like manly working men. Rock and rollers were more peacocks, all very Carnaby Street and Granny Takes A Trip. Will was an early adapter of that peacock finery—all of them in Windhollow were. When I first saw them at the Slade, he was wearing floppy suede boots and a pirate shirt. No gold earring, I think Bowie was the first to do that.

Anyhow, Will was very striking and a real catch. If you were an art student in those days it was very cool to have a musician boyfriend. And I wasn't so bad myself! I was jealous of Arianna, of course, but she was gone so quickly it scarcely mattered.

It's sad now to think of it. We might have been friends, Arianna and I. But that was pre-women's lib, at least for me—my consciousness had yet to expand. We could be very immature, fighting over a bloke: he's mine, no he's mine. I didn't do much of that, but I'm ashamed to say I thought it, even with Lesley.

But only at first. Les was always one of the lads. She could drink anyone under the table, and did. We became good friends, Les and I; lost touch over the years but we never fell out or anything like that. I'd love to see her again.

Will and I hit it off from the start. He didn't give me much cause to be jealous. There were groupies in the folk scene but it wasn't like rock and roll, with fourteen-year-old girls jumping all over you.

Still, I was put off when they all went down to Hampshire for the summer. Their manager, Tom Haring, made it clear that I would not be welcome, and neither would anyone else who wasn't part of the band. Will and I talked every weekend, and he came up to London once, just for the night. I didn't go down until they'd been there about a month. I think it was around the end of June.

Now I can't say this without sounding all, you know, woo-woo. But there was a very, very weird vibe at Wylding Hall. I'm sensitive to that kind of thing. You can laugh all you want but I'm a professional psychic, and I've managed to make a very good living from it for the last thirty years.

Wylding Hall was a bad scene. Or, no, scratch that. "Bad" isn't the right word. We're not talking good and evil, Christian morality, sort of thing. This went much deeper than that. There was a sense of *wrongness*, of things being out of balance—again, not something you would necessarily be aware of if you were just to walk into the house. No overturned furniture or broken glass, nothing like that. Just the normal amount of mess you'd expect in a group house where a bunch of teenagers and twenty-year-olds were living. That's how old I was—twenty—lest you think I was some mad old woman skulking about.

But as soon as I walked into that old house, I could tell something was wrong. Even before I arrived, I knew. I'd caught a ride from London as far as Farnham, then hitchhiked the rest of the way. Got picked up by a lovely old man who was a farmer in the village there, he supplied them with food, driving a truck that seemed as old as he was.

"Going to Muck Manor, then?" he asked. "Hop in. I'm going there myself."

He had a basket of eggs and veg he was bringing down to the folks at Wylding Hall. It was a lucky thing for me—I would never have found the place by myself, and his was the only car I saw the whole time I was there. He was very friendly, not at all the old man shaking his fist that Ashton makes him out to be. His wife had died a few years before and I think he was lonely.

But he seemed—not exactly suspicious—but reserved, when it came to everyone at Wylding Hall. I don't even think it was them so much as the fact that they were staying at the house. He and Will actually got on very well, Will told me after, and I saw that when the farmer dropped me off. Mr. Thomas, that was his name. Really just a lovely old man.

He told me they should be careful what they got up to at the house. I thought he meant they'd all been smoking dope or hash, which certainly they would have been. I told him not to worry, things like that were sure to be exaggerated, besides which cannabis wasn't really a drug but a medicinal herb. See, I was ahead of my time in that, too.

"None of my business what they put in their pipes," he said, "or down their throats. But that lad keeps walking in the woods? He should be careful."

I said, "The gingery one?" I assumed he meant Will. I was just starting to get very much into earth magic, and Will and I had talked about how much it tied into some of the older music he was tracking down.

But he meant Julian. "No, the tall lad, the one whose face you can't see for his hair, the one who won't talk. I see him in the woods when I'm out after the milking, before sun's up. Looking at trees and stones."

"There can't be anything wrong with *that*," I said. I was a bit surprised—I thought maybe Jon had gone off with a guy from the village or Ashton had brought in some girl, or they'd had a bonfire and been boozing and making a row singing. That sort of thing.

But the old man was adamant. "He should stay away from the wood. All of them. There's old stone walls there and pits, they'll take a fall and kill themselves. Get lost if the mist comes over."

"Well, I'll be sure and tell them to be careful."

"Care won't do it. Care killed the cat."

There was no point arguing, so I changed the subject. He was perfectly friendly when he dropped me off. Will came running out, and Les and the rest of them, everyone happy to see me. Julian too; he was very cheerful, laughed and took the basket from Mr. Thomas and thanked him. Mr. Thomas didn't say a thing, didn't blink an eye or look askance. Everyone was perfectly cheerful and good-natured and loose, the farmer stood around chatting for a bit and then he drove off in that claptrap truck.

As soon as he left, I could feel it. It was a beautiful day, bright sunlight and very hot, everything smelling of sun and roses from the overgrown bushes in front of the house, gorgeous blood-red roses; they hadn't been trimmed back in years.

But I felt a sort of paralysing cold. Not from the wind: it was as though my body had suddenly turned to cold metal. I couldn't move, couldn't talk; just stood there staring out the drive toward the trees.

Yet the sun remained, and the butterflies hovering above the flowers, and Will and the rest all laughing and going through the basket to see what the farmer had brought them.

It was so cold I literally could not move. I couldn't even shiver, or uncurl my fingers. You know the saying, "my blood froze"?

Well, this was far worse than that; worse than anything I could imagine. It was as though my entire body had frozen solid. I couldn't breathe. Couldn't blink. Couldn't hear a thing, not them talking or the wind or the truck driving off or bees. Couldn't scream out to Will to help me or to anyone else, all of them talking and going on as though I wasn't even there.

And that was when I realised: This is what it's like to be dead. No clouds or lights or bright tunnel, not even darkness: just the world turning and going on without you and you'll never be part of it again.

I screamed then—really screamed, so loud they all jumped and Lesley let out a shriek and I saw her face go white.

"Nancy!" Will rushed over and grabbed me. I was sobbing and couldn't talk, just gasped as I tried to catch my breath. "Are you all right? What happened?"

I shook my head. *I don't know, I don't know*—that's all I could say. Will looked at the others, and they all stared at me until at last he walked me inside and sat me down in the front room. After a few minutes it was clear I wasn't going to keel over dead, and at that point everyone loosened up and began to laugh.

I did too—not a very convincing laugh, but I'd given them a shock and I felt bad about it. Lesley pulled over a chair and sat beside me.

"What was that, Nancy? A sort of fit?"

I shook my head, finally nodded. "Yes, no, I don't know. Maybe."

"Here." She pulled out a flask of whiskey and handed it to me. "This will help what ails you."

That was her answer to everything. But at that moment, I was glad to take it.

Will

Well, Nance fancied herself a witch in those days. Her and half the girls in London. She's the only one I knew made a career of it, though.

Tom

I'm still angry about that. I blame her for some of what happened. Putting ideas in their heads, especially Julian. That's why I wanted them down there, for God's sake, to avoid outside influences.

And I think what she does now is shameful—taking money from ignorant people, people who want to believe in...well, whatever the hell it is they want to believe in. Like Harry Houdini getting duped by all those spiritualists because he was so desperate to get a message from his dead mother. I'm glad she's in Florida or wherever it is she lives now. I wouldn't trust myself if I ran into her in the street.

Jon

No one put any ideas in our heads. Not mine anyway. Certainly not Nancy. I know that Tom holds it against her that she came down that weekend, but really, what did that have to do with anything that happened later?

Truth is, there was something in the air back then. There really was. Things just felt different in those days, and not just at Wylding Hall, but everywhere. You could sense it, like a smell, or a certain way the light came down through the trees. Everything looked golden. Everything *felt* golden. Like anything could happen.

Wylding Hall intensified all that. It was like a lens: you focus the light through it, ordinary sunlight, but the lens intensifies it, makes it strong enough to start a fire.

We had a game we'd play sometimes at Wylding Hall, after we'd had a good day and night of rehearsing and smoked a few spliffs—Julian got very good hash from a bloke in Notting Hill. We'd all hold our hands and shut our eyes. Then, without speak-ing, we'd drop our hands, and one at a time we'd open our eyes. All without talking. We thought that maybe, just maybe, if we did it at the right moment, in the right place, with the right people, we'd open our eyes and we'd be somewhere else.

I don't know where. Just someplace we'd never been. Some impossible place. It never worked. Not with me, anyway. I was never that stoned. Sometimes I wish I had been.

Will

I think what it was, Julian and Nance were the canaries in the coal mine for that place. They were sensitives—not *sensitive*, though they were that, but people who can sense things that other people don't. Psychics I guess you'd call them, thought that's probably not the right term, either. Julian was certainly very conscious of any kind of emotional distress or tension between all of us in the band, especially once we were at Wylding Hall.

There was a sort of balance we tried to maintain, consciously or not, and I respect Tom for doing what he did, arranging for us to have that place to ourselves for three months. In retrospect, it wasn't a good thing. It was a disaster.

But we weren't to know that, and I don't think anyone can be blamed, certainly not Nance. She does have a gift, whatever you choose to call it. She was very strong, much stronger than Julian. So if the two of them were the canaries in the coal mine, she was perhaps the one who felt it first, but she got out quickly—she was only there that one weekend.

Julian withstood it much longer. People forget that the colliers didn't just bring the canaries into the mines to warn them against the poisonous gases. They took them down because they sang so beautifully, even in the dark.

Lesley

She had a seizure of some kind. I was looking right at her when it happened. Silas Thomas had picked her up hitchhiking and given her a ride. The boys all ran to see what he'd brought for us, and I was rushing over to Nancy. We'd met a couple of times and hit it off, and I was craving female companionship. A fortnight in the woods with only lads takes it out of you.

Really, I was just looking forward to having a laugh, the two of us gossiping and catching up on what was going on back in London. She tumbled out of the truck, looked around smiling—it was a gorgeous day, that whole summer I don't think it rained once. She just stood there, staring into the air and smiling, the way you do when you first arrive from the city and breathe in country air; kind of blissed out.

Then she let out this blood-curdling scream. *Truly* blood-curdling—it was like she was being murdered right there in front of us.

I just about jumped out of my skin and took off running, that's how scared I was. But Nancy only stood there, screaming with her eyes wide open.

She looked like she was asleep. Have you ever seen someone who's having a night terror? Not a nightmare—a night terror is when you think you're awake. Your eyes are open and you see things that aren't there. Will has them sometimes, ever since that summer.

Nancy looked like that. But she wasn't asleep. It was the middle of the afternoon and she was as wide awake as I am now. I ran over and grabbed her and brought her inside, sat her down. Will got her something to drink. I held her hands and kept talking to her, the way you do a spooked horse.

Her hands were freezing—so cold that when I touched her, it hurt. Burned, the way that cold iron burns. You know stories about kids putting each other to licking a flagpole in winter? This is how I imagined that would feel—not that I was licking her.

And it really *did* burn me. Right there, those white marks—that's where I touched her. It blistered, hurt like hell for a few days. When it finally healed, I was left with that scar.

Still, we quickly got over Nancy's fit. Will took her up to bed and shagged her and that put her to rights. You couldn't sneeze in that place without everyone knowing it.

We had a party that night, stayed up till two or three a.m., singing and dancing. Nancy was a wonderful dancer. "Saint Dominic's Preview" had just come out and she'd brought it down. "Jackie Wilson Said", we played that over and over again. It was a big deal when a new record came out, you'd buy it then find one of your mates who had a stereo and everyone would come over to listen to it together for the first time.

We had several record players at Wylding Hall—Julian had one, and Jon, and I think Ashton. They were expensive, as were albums. Jon had brought his turntable to the rehearsal room and that's where we'd play whatever we were listening to, so everyone could hear it.

That night it was Van Morrison. Sexy music, everyone was feeling very friendly. Hormones running at high tide. Nothing like adding a new face to the mix to spice things up. That's where the rumours of orgies came from, that one night. God knows who started them, I know I never said anything. It must have been Nancy when she went back to London. No, my lips remain sealed.

Nancy

There was no orgy. It was all very innocent. We ended up on the floor, that's all, stoned and lying on our backs with our hands touching. This game they played in the dark; it was the shank of the night, and we closed our eyes and just lay there, breathing.

After a while someone began to sing. It was the most haunting song. No words, just a melody.

I could never recall it afterward, but it was something I never forgot. It's true. I can hear it sometimes, still—it's there in my head and I can't get it out. I thought it was Julian. But he said no, he wasn't singing. But he heard it, too.

Jon

It was definitely a male voice—a boy's. Someone whose voice hadn't yet broken. Julian had a reedy voice but this was a true boy's soprano. It made the hair on my neck stand up. I couldn't make out the words.

Ashton

We were all fucking stoned out of our minds, that's all. We'd been playing and singing earlier, and then Jon put on that damned Van Morrison album and left it so it just played over and over and over again. Everyone finally just zonked out on the floor, at some point the stereo got turned off and we fell asleep. Someone dreamed they heard singing. I think Lesley was singing in her sleep. It happens. Anyway, there was no one else there, no... ghost, or whatever they say.

Yeah, I heard something. Like, I said, it was Lesley. Didn't sound like her but it was. Definitely a woman's voice.

Definitely not Nancy. She couldn't carry a tune in a bucket.

Lesley

It wasn't me, because I wasn't asleep, and I heard it too. I thought it was Will—gorgeous tenor, almost a counter tenor, a bit of a quaver in it. A very eerie melody. Like the Abbots Bromley Horn Dance. Will collected old tunes like that, and I suppose that's why I assumed it was him. He refuses to talk about it.

Julian heard it. I asked him the next morning, had he heard the singing. We had stumbled off to bed together but we didn't have sex. He didn't say anything. He pretended not to hear me. That was when it ended between the two of us, not that it had ever really started.

The thing that disturbed me about that night in the rehearsal room wasn't the singing; we all heard that, even if some won't talk about it. It was afterward. We were all still lying on the floor in the big room. People were asleep. I know Ashton was asleep because he snores, and Will was too.

Julian was beside me. He wasn't sleeping, but he wanted me to think he was asleep. I touched his hand, ran my fingers along his arm; nothing.

I felt horrible. If he'd rejected me outright or if we'd had a fight, I could understand that. But he was just freezing me out, and I was utterly obsessed with him—crazy, the way you are when you're seventeen. I thought I would die, I was so in love with him. But it was like loving a book, or a beautiful song; something you could never really touch.

He was on the floor beside me, and Nancy was next to him. All of a sudden I felt this insane jealousy, just on fire—he wanted to be with her! That's why he wasn't responding to me.

So I lay there and held my breath, to hear if they were whispering to each other, or if they were touching. I imagined her hand on him and I couldn't see and it was driving me crazy.

I couldn't hear a thing. It was pitch dark, a few weeks past midsummer so it was still bright till almost ten at night, and the sun rose very early. But that night it seemed as though it stayed dark hours longer than it should have. I just lay there, creepy little me, listening to their breathing and to hear if Nancy was having him off.

I didn't hear a peep. Until finally Julian whispered, "I saw it too."

I thought he was talking to me, but he was so quiet I thought maybe he was talking to himself. Talking in his sleep.

But then I heard Nancy move, very, very slightly—she must have turned her head towards his—and I heard her whisper, "*I know.*"

That was all. I kept holding my breath in case they went on, but there was nothing else. I never asked Julian about it. Like I said, the next day, whatever was between us was over.

I was heartbroken but I didn't show it—didn't want anyone to think it mattered. We all had mayfly relationships in those days. Girls did, anyway. You'd be with someone for a one-night stand and it was like you were engaged to be married, you'd be so excited.
But it was over. I didn't know much back then, but I knew that whatever had happened between Julian and me was done. I have no idea what they were talking about, him and Nancy. I have no idea what they saw.

Nancy

Suddenly I heard this uncanny singing. To this day I can't explain what it was. Less like singing than birdsong, quite high-pitched, almost piercing; then a series of trills, and that high keening again. Then a fluttering sound right above me, like something was trapped in the rafters.

I knew we weren't supposed to open our eyes, but I couldn't help it. When I heard that rustling noise, my eyes popped right open. I almost bolted. I thought it was rats scurrying around, which wouldn't have surprised me a bit. There were all sorts of things living in the walls there. Rats and mice and God knows what.

So there I am, staring at the ceiling—and that's when I realise it can't possibly be rats. Whatever it is, it's *above* me. The rehearsal room had very high ceilings, which should have made for a bad acoustic, but didn't. It sounded like a bird had got in and was bashing itself against the beams up there, trying to get out.

I started to sit up but I felt Julian's hand on my arm, holding me back. He didn't say anything, not out loud, but I knew he was telling me to stay beside him and look at the ceiling. Like he was a transmitter and I was picking up the frequency he was on.

I looked up, but I couldn't see anything. It was pitch dark, darker even than it had seemed when my eyes were shut. The bird kept flying back and forth, I could hear it strike the beams and the ceiling.

A hollow thump, over and over again.

There was something horrible about it. The fact that it just kept bashing itself against the beams and wouldn't stop: it was killing itself, trying to get out. And if it *did* fall, it would fall on me, and that would be even more horrible.

Even with Julian trying to hold me back, I knew I had to get away. I tried to sit up, but it was like when I'd first arrived. I couldn't move, couldn't speak, couldn't breathe. And all the while that bird is thrashing about, and Julian beside me is breathing faster and faster—it was almost like he was getting off on it.

At some point the bird stopped flying. It must have found its way out, because I didn't hear it fall. That was when the singing began again, the same eerie song I'd heard before.

Only now Julian sang along with it, so softly that I couldn't hear any words. I have no idea if he was just chanting, or if he was trying to make contact with something—if he'd entered some sort of liminal state. You know, in-between; here and not-here. It's what I do for a living, but I've trained myself over the decades. And I'm always very careful, because it can be extremely dangerous.

With Julian, I think he was like a kid playing with electricity; fiddling with the wireless, touching the electric fence to get a little shock. Without knowing it, he grabbed a live wire, and—*pffft*. Maybe that's how the bird found its way out. It wasn't until long after that it struck me, maybe it wasn't trying to find a way out at all. Maybe it was trying to find a way in.

Will

Things got much more intense after the weekend Nance came down. It was like all the sexual tension and creative energy somehow got focussed, and what it got focussed on was the songs. I was definitely in a better state, because I'd spent the weekend with my girlfriend, so I knew where *my* sexual energy had gone.

Les and Julian broke up then. I'm not sure what happened, but I never had the impression that sex was as important to Julian as it was to some of us. That changed when the girl showed up, but that was later.

After that weekend, Les seemed pretty upset. She was trying to act like nothing had happened between her and Julian, that it didn't matter. But you could just tell, she was very hurt.

Les always comes off as one of the lads—that's her defence mechanism; swaggering about like she owns the room she's in. You know, tough little bird, swears like a sailor, drink us all under the table— well, that part's true.

But the rest of it, that's just a defence. No one could go through what we did and come out the other side without being affected by it. I eventually had to stop drinking if I was to survive. Ashton has always been a hard contrary bastard, and Wylding Hall just made him harder. But everyone deals with it differently.

Patricia Kenyon, journalist

I first heard about the scene at Wylding Hall from Nancy
O'Neill. We were friends, not especially close but we hung out in
the same circles. I had recently started writing for *NME*—I was one
of the first women rock journalists; it was a real boys' club in those
days, Nick Kent and all the rest, and I had to spend way too much
time boozing and drugging with the boys to prove myself.

So I was always happy to have a girl's night out. There was a party at the Marquee, very bisexual chic—boys with boys, girls with
girls, everyone with everyone. I wasn't out of the closet then—I was
twenty and still living at home—and I felt a bit intimidated by how
open some of those people were. Nancy was straight, so she was my
beard—I could be with her and everyone would think we were a
couple, and I wouldn't have to worry about the fact that I was, you
know, *actually gay.*

So we go off into a corner with a bottle of champers and get to
talking and I asked her how things were with Will Fogerty; were
they still going out? The truth is I kind of fancied Nancy—sounds
like a song, right? And I thought, well, maybe if she's broken up with
Will...

But she hadn't. Not yet, anyway. Instead she starts telling me
about this bizarre weekend she'd just had down in Hampshire, at a
ruined country house called Wylding Hall. Tom Haring had locked
up everyone in the band Windhollow Faire, and he wouldn't let
them out till they'd finished an album. I laughed.

"What, like locking a bunch of monkeys in a room with type-
writers until one of them writes Shakespeare?"

"I'm serious, Tricia. It was seriously...strange."

Of course that was all it took for me to immediately want to see
for myself exactly what was going on. I knew Windhollow's first
album—it had come out late the previous year, featured on John
Peel and BBC Radio One, half-page advert in *Rolling Stone*, blah
blah blah. Everything you could expect from an electric folk album.
There weren't many venues for music reviews then, so there wasn't
the sort of coverage they might have gotten today.

It wasn't a groundbreaking album, not like *Wylding Hall* was when it was released. Still, people were talking about Windhollow Faire. Today we'd call it buzz. I'd seen them perform once at UFO. Not the ideal hall for them, I thought; too big and everyone was totally out of their mind on acid. I was so square, I found all the noise and whirling around in ponchos kind of distracting. Going down to Hampshire and sitting in on rehearsals in a stately home seemed like a good angle for me to pitch an article for *NME*. Easier said than done.

"Put that right out of your pointy little head," Nancy told me when I brought it up. "Tom Haring's got his knickers in a twist over me going there. He rang me up and said if I told anyone where they were that he'd slap a cease and desist order on me."

I was incredulous. "That's absurd. He can't do that and you know it."

Nancy was silent. Finally she said, "Maybe. But I don't think you should go, either. It gave me a bad feeling."

"All the more reason for me to go! Things fall apart, the centre of the folk scene cannot hold, sort of thing. That would make a great piece."

She was adamant. Wouldn't give me the phone number at the house, wouldn't even tell me the name of the village. Nowadays you could just Google it, but I had nothing to go on. I asked around but no one seemed to know. There were a lot of rumours, but I couldn't afford to be driving around the English countryside looking for musicians laying low somewhere in Hampshire. Everyone and his dog was living in a commune by then—hippies, anarchists, Luddites, aristos. I finally called Tom Haring.

"Absolutely not," he shouted, and hung up on me. I called back and he hung up again. It took me five tries before we even had a civil conversation. After that, it was days of me hectoring him before he gave in and agreed to let me go down there.

"We can time the piece so it comes out right when the album does," I told him. "It will be great publicity."

"Will you give me right of refusal if I don't agree with what you say?"

Now it was my turn to dig in my heels. "Absolutely not. Have you run this by the band?"

"In fact I have. They're gun-shy about journalists after all the bad press about Arianna. And they're at a very delicate place in their creative process."

Their creative process. What a load of bollocks! I just kept at him, and eventually I wore him down.

"Look, Tom, you know that even bad publicity's better than none. Not that this will be bad," I assured him. "I'm genuinely fascinated by their creative process and by the entire band, especially Julian Blake."

"You and everyone else."

Eventually Tom relented. I could go, but only for the day, and only if he accompanied me. No overnight stays, at the house or in the village. Which was a moot point—there was no place to stay within twenty miles. Wylding Hall was at the end of the fucking earth.

"Picking Up the Pieces: Windhollow Faire's Remarkable Rural Revival," by Patricia Kenyon

New Musical Express, January 17, 1972

You enter Wylding Hall as into a dream, or perhaps a time machine.

First there's the anteroom, filled with coats and wellies, muddy trainers and the odd Fair Isle jumper or velvet cape. Oh, and a cricket bat. Then a whitewashed corridor, walls hung with ancient photographs of prize pigs and family members long deceased, slate floor strewn with rushes as it might have been a thousand years ago. From here one finds the kitchen, where the Twentieth Century finally begins to hold sway—running water, a gas range and refrigerator—but only briefly.

"The beating heart of Wylding Hall is this way." Will Fogerty, the band's fiddle player and resident musicologist, beck-

ons me down a few stone steps worn from centuries of human traffic.

"Watch yourself," he adds, a bit too late as I've already banged my head on a wooden beam.

As we now know, an encounter with the beating heart of Wylding Hall leaves no one unscathed, even—or especially— the members of Windhollow Faire. But on this idyllic mid- summer morning, one can hardly imagine a lovelier place than this 16th century manor house, with its late Victorian addi- tions and all mod cons in the rehearsal hall where Windhol- low has parked its instruments and sound equipment, along with Indian-print tapestries, Turkish carpets, brass hookah and hi-fi system with an advance pressing of Todd Rundgren's Something/Anything *on the turntable.*

"We've been playing that one nonstop," Will says, running a hand through a thatch of auburn hair. "Brilliant produc- tion."

The sun slants through the high windows. The sweet smell of beeswax polish mingles with that of ganja and the black Sobranie cigarettes favoured by one of the band members.

Will steps over a heap of Navajo blankets that turns out to be Julian Blake. Julian rubs the sleep from his eyes and blinks at us, more Alice's Dormouse than the eighteen-year-old gui- tar prodigy responsible for writing most of the songs for their album-in-progress.

"Oh, hello," Julian greets us with a yawn. "Is it morning? Or still yesterday?"

It's all rather as if a hippy caravan has taken over the maze at Hampton Court...

Patricia

To me, it was very apparent that there was something off about Julian. I'd seen him once before, performing with Windhollow at the Marquee, and he made a real impression on me. Very tall, very good looking, sort of a delicately handsome face. The young Jeremy

Irons might have played him. He was a finger picker, which was unusual for a guitarist, at least in rock music.

And he had eccentric tunings. He'd taught himself, and while he read music, I always had the impression he was someone who played more by ear.

That morning at Wylding Hall he seemed to be in a different place, mentally. He was the one who chain-smoked those horrible Russian cigarettes. The smell was everywhere. His fingers were stained yellow—a real, jaundiced yellow—and they were so long, they looked like great spiders' legs clutching at that Indian blanket.

He didn't look like someone who'd just woken up. He looked... manic; eyes a little too wide. He laughed when he saw me and shook his head, then just kept staring at me, as though waiting for me to recognise that he'd made a joke.

But he hadn't said anything. It was unnerving. He reminded me of Syd Barrett. *Oh God,* I thought, *another fucking acid casualty.* I said hello and he laughed again and wandered off, draped in his blanket like Lear on the heath. Will toddled after him, to make us some tea.

That left me alone in the room. Down on the floor, Julian had left this nest of blankets. When I bent to examine it, I found a copy of *Alice in Wonderland,* open to the Mad Tea Party.

> Alice had been looking over his shoulder with some curiosity. "What a funny watch!" she remarked. "It tells the day of the month, and doesn't tell what o'clock it is!"
>
> "Why should it?" muttered the Hatter. "Does your watch tell you what year it is?"
>
> "Of course not," said Alice very readily: "but that's because it stays the same year for such a long time together."
>
> "Which is just the case with mine," said the Hatter.
>
> Alice felt dreadfully puzzled. The Hatter's remark seemed to have no sort of meaning in it, and yet it was certainly English. "I don't quite understand you," she said, as politely as she could.
>
> "The Dormouse is asleep again," said the Hatter, and he poured a little hot tea upon its nose.

Tucked in among the blankets were several more books, not much bigger than a Moleskin notebook, which is what I thought they were at first. I looked around to make sure the others were gone, then knelt and looked through them.

They weren't notebooks at all but very old books, in leather covers. One was done up in vellum and written in very archaic English. Another was in Latin.

I felt excited but also uneasy. I'd done classics at uni and I knew what these were—books of magic. The one in Old English was a grimoire. A scrap of notebook paper fell out of it, covered with writing in biro. Julian's writing, I knew that without being told; a spidery hand to suit those spidery fingers.

I thought he'd copied out a spell. Later, when I heard the *Wylding Hall* album, I realised it was an old ballad by Thomas Campion—a song in the form of a spell, dating to the 15th century.

> *Thrice tosse these Oaken ashes in the ayre;*
> *Thrice sit though mute in this inchained chayre:*
> *And thrice three times tye up this true loves knot,*
> *And murmur soft shee will, or shee will not.*
> *Goe burn these poys'nous weedes in yon blew fire,*
> *These Screeche-owles fethers, and this prickling bryier,*
> *This Cypresse gathered at a dead mans grave;*
> *That all thy feares and cares an end may have.*

I thought I heard voices, so I dropped everything and scrambled back to my feet. But no one came, and when I listened I could tell they were in the kitchen with Will. I knew he wanted to go over some of the details about studio time.

I figured they might be a while, and this might be a good time to do a bit of exploring on my own, without someone at my shoulder steering me past whatever it was I wasn't supposed to be looking at. This is why you have to be very careful when you invite a journalist into your midst.

The big room where they rehearsed was in one of the newer sections of the farmhouse, 18th century, tacked onto the Victorian addition. Tom had told me that the original manor was Tudor, and parts of it were older than that, fourteenth century.

So I did a bit of exploring. Their bedrooms were all in the newer wing, and I knew these would be off-limits to me. But one of the doors from the rehearsal room opened onto a hallway, and I followed that.

The place was immense. From outside, you just had no idea of the scale. It was originally a manor house, where a knight would have lived—you could see where the old part began because the walls changed, from wood and plaster to herringbone brick, with massive oaken joists and beams.

The hall grew narrower as I wandered along. Diamond-paned windows, that beautiful leaded glass that catches the light and throws it back in rainbows, like a prism. There were crooked wooden doors, oak planks banded with iron, so heavy and warped I couldn't open most of them.

And of course I tried—who wouldn't? The ones I could open seemed to have been used as storerooms for the last few hundred years, dank and musty and dark. I wasn't going to start poking around in them.

So I kept going, until I found a stone stairway and climbed to the next floor. It was so dark I kept my hand on the wall the whole time, to make sure I didn't lose my footing. I couldn't see my hand in front of my face, and the passage was so narrow my shoulders brushed the walls. It was like climbing into my own tomb.

I'd forgotten my watch, and so I lost all track of time. But finally I reached the top of the stairs and stepped out onto a landing. There to one side was an open door. Light poured into the hall, and it took a moment for my eyes to adjust before I walked in.

It was a library—a very, very old library. You're supposed to keep books out of the light, but this room must have been at least five hundred years old, built at a time when you'd want—need—natural light to read properly. Assuming you were literate and *could* read.

I've never been in such a beautiful room; dark oak walls with carved linen-fold panelling, hand-carved bookshelves, and a row of diamond-paned windows, with leaves blown against them on the outside so that the light that filtered down seemed to come from a forest canopy. One of the windows must have been broken—there were leaves scattered across the floor, green willow and birch.

And there was a fireplace big enough to walk into, filled knee-high with grey ash. The room smelled of wood smoke: when I held my hands above the ashes, the air felt warm. Someone had been burning something.

Another odd thing was the walls. When I first walked into the library, I assumed the panelled walls were linen-fold—what you usually find in posh houses of that vintage. But when I looked closer, I saw the panelling was carved like overlapping feathers—there must have been thousands of them. Not big peacock feathers, either: small feathers, about the size of your thumbnail. The detail was extraordinary, you could see every quill and the wood was so smooth it felt like silk.

The bookshelves were carved, too, with a repeating pattern of twigs and leaves with a little bird like a sparrow worked in here and there. You had to look carefully to find the birds, they were so small and carefully concealed within the larger pattern. The shelves weren't filled, but there were still a lot of books—several hundred at least. Not very orderly. It looked like a library used often by the same person, someone who always knew where to find whatever book he wanted to put his hands on.

There were more books on a table by the window, in a language I couldn't make out. Arabic, maybe? I can't remember, it's been so long. And another grimoire, not much bigger than my hand. It was in good nick, the leather cover very soft. The pages felt stiff and new. The ink looked new as well, not at all faded; black ink, not that dull brown you find in most very old books.

And this book was very old. I'm no expert, but even I could tell it must have been written around the time this wing was built. When I opened it, I swear I could smell fresh ink. I looked at the frontispiece for a date or name, but found nothing.

I did come across a bookmark—a birch leaf that had been picked within the last day or so, still green. Beneath it was a fragment of manuscript covered with writing, so old it crumbled when I touched it. I had my notebook with me—I'm a journalist, remember—and I quickly began to copy out the writing word for word. I thought it might make good copy.

Burna thyn haer yn flamme
Tiss wrennas fedyr and thyn hatte blod

That's all I got down when I heard someone behind me. I whirled around but there was no one by the door. When I turned back, someone was at the other end of the room, watching me. A very old woman I thought at first, not as tall as me, slight and white-haired. But she wasn't old—it was a trick of the sun in the window above her, bleaching the colour from her hair.

Then I saw that her hair really *was* white—bright as silver, rather mussed-up hair that fell just above her shoulders. She didn't look more than fourteen or fifteen, wearing a plain white dress that came just below her knees. A vintage petticoat, the kind of hippy frock that girls snapped up at Portobello Road. Strange tawny eyes. She took a step toward me and stopped. She looked surprised, as though she'd been expecting someone else.

"What are you doing here?"

I jumped: it was a man's voice. And it didn't come from her but from the door, where Julian stood, staring at me. I couldn't tell if he was angry or just confused.

I said, "Nothing," and glanced back at the girl.

But she was gone.

Tom

It was a good article, what Patricia Kenyon wrote for *NME*—a very good piece. Unfortunately, by the time it appeared that autumn, we were all focussed on damage control. The album had to come out on schedule and there was a tour all lined up, shows in London and Brighton. I was in the last stages of booking them in the U.S. around the holidays. The rumour mill had been running for a few months by then. Patricia's article did a lot to calm that down, put things into perspective. I suspect she could have caused us a lot of trouble if she'd wanted to.

But that was never her intent, with us or anyone else. She's a brilliant writer, one of the best. Deserves every bit of praise she's ever received. In retrospect it was extremely fortunate that I let her go down there, much as I was dead set against the idea at first. She became a sort of witness for the defence, long after the fact.

Patricia

Afterward, I thought she must've been his girlfriend, the one he met in the pub. I never met her and there aren't any photos, other than the cover for Wylding Hall. But from the description, that's who it must have been. Right?

Lesley

Julian was into black magic. Well, okay—he never called it that. But something to do with the dark arts. "Magick" with a K, that Aleister Crowley bullshit. So fucking pretentious. Most of Crowley's quote-unquote magick was just a way of getting laid—he was a total con man. If you can read his stuff with a straight face, you're a stronger woman than me.

Julian wasn't like that. He was interested in the nature of time. The only thing he loved more than his guitar was that fancy wristwatch of his, with all the dials and arrows and whatnot. He loved to play with it, winding it back and forth and watching the hands turn. Like a kid. I think he actually believed that he could control time.

Or no, it's more like he believed there were other *kinds* of time; that you could step out of our ordinary time, and into another one. Like Rip Van Winkle. Julian was fascinated by those kind of stories. He must've pulled every book off the shelves at Wylding Hall, looking for them. Before we even went to Wylding Hall, he'd asked Will to search for ballads like that at Cecil Sharp House. There aren't many, so Julian made up his own. That's what his version of the Campion song was.

Spells, that's what Julian was trying to write. He wouldn't cop to it, but I knew he was up to something. I'd knock and knock at the door, he wouldn't answer so I'd let myself in.

He wouldn't even know I was there. He'd stand in the middle of the floor with his eyes closed, talking to himself. I'd speak to him, and even if I touched him, he wouldn't react. This would go on for minutes. When he'd finally snap out of it and open his eyes, they'd dilate—but not like a normal person's eyes. More like an owl's: one second they were all pupil, and then suddenly they'd shrink to almost nothing.

The first time it happened, I almost jumped out of my skin. I screamed and grabbed him, and it was like pulling a bed sheet from a piano. I could barely feel his arm between my fingers.

He just—*crumpled* and fell to the floor. Like his bones had dissolved. I thought he was dead. But after a minute he blinked and his eyes seemed to focus, and I knew he could see me. He started yelling that I'd ruined it, he'd almost done it and I'd fucked it all up, whatever "it" was.

That happened, what? Three times, maybe four. Those are just the times I know of, when I walked into his room or came on him when he was out in the woods and saw it for myself.

I don't think it was drugs. That's the obvious answer, I know. But I've seen so many people strung out on heroin or whatever, and this was different. His eyes—I've only ever seen one other person whose eyes went like that.

Yeah, her. Guessed it in one.

Will

There's probably a hundred variations on the wren carol. Different words, different melodies. God knows where Julian found the one he sang. He never went to Cecil Sharp House, not as far as I know.

And he never asked me about the songs I found there, or anywhere else, which got my back up somewhat. I didn't expect the others to appreciate what I was doing, not from an archival perspective. But Julian, you'd think this was exactly the sort of thing he'd be interested in. Never said a word to me about it. Whenever I'd ask about the songs he covered, where he found them, why he'd chosen

that particular arrangement, he'd just shrug and say he couldn't remember.

His version of the carol went like this:

We are the boys who come today
To bury the wren on St. Stephen's Day.
Where shall we bury her feathers?
In a grave mound.
What shall we do with her bones?
Bury them in the ground.
They'll break men's plows!
Cast them into the sea.
They'll grow into great rocks
That will wreck ships and boats!
We'll burn them in the fire
And throw her ashes to the sky.

A bit bloodthirsty. You'd be surprised how many old songs are
like that. I was very curious as to where he'd found his variation. I
knew there was a library at Wylding Hall and that Julian spent time
there. In the Tudor wing, he told me.

"It's easy—you go a ways into the Tudor wing, through a long
passage with windows, then up a flight of steps. Stone stairs, I think
that bit's older than the rest. Norman, maybe. Once you reach the
top, the library's on the your right. Can't miss it."

Famous last words. Not only was it possible to miss it, I got so
lost I was afraid I'd never find my way back. The hallway with the
windows was easy enough—very pretty, diamond panes and glimps-
es of the gardens outside.

But after that I must've taken a wrong turn. I walked and walked,
but there was no sign of a stone stairway. Nothing but old storerooms, doors that I couldn't pry open. Dark, too—there weren't
many windows, and the ones I saw were all high up and deeply re-
cessed, so I could see pockets of blue sky but not much else. The
glass might have been broken, or maybe they never had glass in

them at all. Maybe the original structure was even older than Julian thought.

Either way, it was much colder than the rest of Wylding Hall. There was no central heating, of course, not in a heap that old and that big, but the part we stayed in got a lot of sun. And it was summer.

Here it felt more like autumn, or even early winter. Cold enough to see my breath. That freaked me out.

And the wood smelled strange—the timbers that crisscrossed the ceiling and the panelled walls, even the furniture. Everything was made of wood, so the smell was quite noticeable. Not like furniture polish or beeswax; a nasty smell, putrid and slightly sweet. Like roses left in a vase where the water goes all green and scummy. Even now, I don't like to think of it.

I pulled open doors, looking for a stairway or another passage, but I didn't see anything but nearly empty bedrooms with cup-board beds, all so covered with cobwebs it looked like ash.

Finally I just gave up. I stopped and turned and began to retrace my steps.

Immediately I was lost. Nothing looked the same—the windows seemed higher and narrower, and outside the sky looked darker. I could see stars. I know that sounds crazy, but it's true.

Now I was really starting to freak out. Hallways branched off the passage, and I knew I hadn't seen them before, because I was looking for the stairwell. I stopped and listened, but I couldn't hear a sound. No voices. None of the creaking you usually hear in old houses. It wasn't rational, but I grew terrified I wouldn't be able to find my way back at all. Every time I turned a corner, there'd be two or three more passages branching off from the one I was in.

I remembered something I'd once read about the maze at Hampton Court: to find your way out, you should keep one hand on the wall at all times. I had a bandanna tied around my head to keep my hair out of my eyes, paisley silk—Nancy had given it to me for my birthday. I took it off and tied it to a doorknob. If I ended up back there again, I'd know I'd come in circles. I made my best guess as to the correct direction, put my hand on the wall to the right, and started walking.

If my hand hadn't been on the wall, I would have missed it. An alcove so narrow that anyone bigger than me wouldn't have been able to slip inside: the entrance to a stone stairway.

Once inside, I had only to raise my arms slightly to touch the walls. The stone risers were steep, slightly concave in the centre where they'd been worn over the years. Hundreds, even thousands, of people must have walked those steps. I wondered if anyone had been there recently, besides Julian and myself and the other members of Windhollow.

The stairway was lit by a strange ghostly light, just enough to see by. Yet I saw no lamps or windows. It was as though the light seeped from the stone. I crept along, afraid I'd lose my footing and crack my head. The walls pressed in on me, and the air was so cold my chest ached with each breath. It smelled dank and loamy, with a faint reek of rotted wood.

And it was deathly silent. I stopped once and stamped hard as I could on the steps. I heard only a whispery sound, like a falling leaf.

Goddam Julian, I thought. I thought it was some kind of bad joke, that he'd decided to take me down a peg. After five minutes I stopped again, panting, and looked back.

That was a mistake.

Behind me, the passage spiralled down and down, deeper into shadows than I could have imagined, before it winked from sight entirely. My mouth went dry and I clutched at the wall to keep from falling.

It was impossible that I could have climbed that high, impossible that the building could reach such a height, or plunge so deeply into the earth.

But when I turned, heart pounding, the stairs seemed to wind upwards just as endlessly, until they too disappeared. If I continued on, I'd walk into utter darkness. If I turned back, the same black spiral awaited me, coiling down into some unimaginable abyss.

I couldn't budge. The thought of moving even a fraction of an inch, forward or back, made me so dizzy I was afraid I'd pass out.

The steps were far too narrow for me to sit, so I leaned against the wall and tried to calm myself, counting backwards from a hundred.

I'd reached about fifty when I heard it. A voice, so faint I had to hold my breath to be sure I hadn't imagined it. It was the same voice I'd heard the night Nancy was with us and we all held hands in the dark. I couldn't make out any words.

Almost imperceptibly, it grew louder; loud enough that I realised it was singing. I still couldn't understand the words, but after a few minutes I recognised the melody as a song by Thomas Campion.

Whoever was singing seemed to swallow the words: they became a mindless jumble, and try as I might I couldn't recall them, even though the sound was growing closer.

And now I could hear another sound—a kind of slithering, like something being slowly dragged up the steps.

Or something dragging itself. The wordless song went on. The dank air grew putrid, until I gagged and clapped my hand to my mouth.

With that sudden motion I found I could move again—and I did. I raced up those stairs so fast I nearly tripped, gasping and trying not to choke on that smell. Ahead of me the grey light grew brighter, until a silver line sliced through the darkness—the outline of a door.

Behind me, the slithering became a high-pitched rattle that drowned out the wordless song. I reached the top step and flung myself against the door, pounding as I searched for a latch. My fingers closed around a metal spike and I yanked at it, pulling until the door inched open. I angled around to squeeze through.

And I swear to you, the door began to close on me. I clawed at the wood, but it only squeezed more and more tightly.

Then all at once I was on the other side and stumbling down the hall. I didn't stop until I saw my bandanna tied outside a bed-room. I grabbed it and kept on running, through the corridors and down the stairs to the rehearsal room.

Ashton nearly had a heart attack when I burst inside.

"What the hell are you doing?" he yelled, but I just slammed the door shut and pulled a chair in front of it. I wouldn't talk until he found a bottle of whiskey and shoved it at me. When I *could* talk, I gave him some bollocks about needing to use the telephone for an urgent call. Of course by the time I drank half the bottle and managed to calm myself down, I forgot all about the telephone. Took me the rest of the day before I felt anything like myself again and could pick up my guitar.

I never told Ashton what really happened, or anyone else. At first I was afraid they'd laugh at me. Later I was afraid they'd be angry I hadn't told them sooner. I never told anyone, till now.

Nancy

I wish Lesley had told me what was going on with Julian. Eventually she did, but it was months later. I know that they all scoff at what I do, but Julian didn't. I was the only one who might have been able to talk to him—we were on a similar wavelength, we shared a lot of the same interests. Not the occult so much as arcana—antiquarian books, medieval grimoires, Dr. Dee. Books of knowledge. Things like that. If I'd had a better sense of what he was up to, I might have done something to help, especially after that night on the floor when we heard the voice.

As it was, next morning he and I took a long walk in the woods, very early. Everyone else was passed out. I couldn't sleep because Will was snoring—he was a terrible snorer. I kept kicking him but he wouldn't budge, so I finally gave up and went downstairs to make some tea.

Julian was the only one up. I don't think he'd even been asleep—Lesley told me later that some nights he'd only sleep for an hour or two, before he'd go off into the wood.

But now he seemed wide awake, in good spirits but quiet. Thoughtful. We didn't talk about what had happened the night before, when I'd flashed into whatever it was he'd summoned up. We didn't need to. I knew he knew, and he knew I did. It happens like that. Not often, but sometimes.

We had tea and eggs, he had a smoke then asked if I'd like to go for a walk. I wasn't really dressed for a hike, long skirt and suede boots, but in those days I didn't care about things like that.

It was a perfect summer morning, daisies and campion in bloom, skylarks singing. Butterflies everywhere, wood nymphs and orange tips. Even though it was warm, Julian had on his old corduroy jacket, the one you see in all the pictures. The air had that sweet green smell you get before the leaves begin their turn toward autumn. Dew on the ground, everything shone and dazzled. Like walking inside a kaleidoscope—every shade of green you can imagine, and blue sky beyond, tiny birds hopping everywhere.

Julian was singing to himself, "Thrice Tosse These Oaken Ashes." It was the first time I'd ever heard it—this was months before the album came out. He'd set it to his own music, though there were echoes of that eerie melody we'd heard the night before.

Or, not echoes; more like an absence of sound. As though he'd taken all the silences in a piece of music and strung them together.

It was beautiful, but chilling. Much more so than the version on the album. If things had turned out differently, if they'd been able to record more than one take of Julian's voice—maybe then you'd have a true sense of how it was supposed to sound. It made the hairs on my neck stand up.

That was when I remembered what the farmer had said. *He should stay away from the wood. All of them...*

But it was broad daylight, and there were two of us—if me or Julian had fallen or turned an ankle, we'd have been able to manage. Still, that singing unnerved me, and I was glad when he stopped.

There was a path through the wood, not too overgrown. I think deer must have used it, there were red deer in Hampshire then. That was the direction we took. I asked Julian if he'd been that way before, and he said yes.

"There's some ruins." He seemed excited. His face was flushed, and he started laughing. "Wait till you see, it's brilliant."

"Have any of the others been here?"

"Not yet. I wanted to—well, I wanted to keep it secret." He sounded a bit embarrassed. "I know that's childish, but it's such a beautiful place, I didn't want everyone stamping over it. Having a party and leaving their bottles everywhere."

Which sounded sensible enough to me.

'It's just up here," he said after a few minutes. We walked more slowly now. He no longer seemed excited, not reluctant, exactly, but slightly hesitant. I wondered if he was sorry that he'd decided to share his secret with me.

Ahead of us the woods thinned out. There was a copse of alders, odd I thought—alders usually grow near water, and I hadn't seen any streams or ponds since we'd started. Alders and hazel and rowan. As we drew nearer, I saw that they were arranged in a long oval, and in the centre of the oval was a mound—a long barrow. Like a gigantic egg half-buried in the earth, maybe twenty feet long and eight feet high, all overgrown with ferns and wildflowers. Julian stopped a few yards away and gazed up at it.

"Here it is," he said softly.

He turned and held out his hand. And that was unheard of for Julian—the one thing I knew about him, other than that he was supposed to be a brilliant musician, was that he didn't like to be touched. I flattered myself by thinking maybe he fancied me. Uh oh, I thought, now there'll be trouble with Will and Lesley both.

I took his hand and clambered up after him. Almost immediately I regretted it—the mound was much steeper than it appeared. From ground level, it seemed barely taller than the trees, and some of the bigger ones, oaks and beech, towered above it.

Yet the instant I began climbing, I started to slide backwards. My long skirt made it worse. It took two or three tries before I got any momentum, and if Julian hadn't been holding on to me, I don't think I could have done it. The turf was ankle-high, very soft but slick as glass, with bluebells and narcissus peeking out of it, even though the season for bluebells was long gone. The grass smelled sweet where we crushed it, and everywhere wrens darted out from their nests in the brush. There must have been a hundred of them. Wrens don't fly very high, so they skimmed all around us, singing then disappearing into the tangle underfoot. I've never seen so many birds.

It took a good five minutes to reach the top. When we did, I was so out of breath I couldn't say a word. Julian immediately let go of my hand.

"Look at this!" He sounded giddy, spinning in a circle with his arms out. "You can see for miles!"

I looked around, and gasped.

Everywhere I turned, there was the countryside. Fields and woods and roadways, villages like clusters of acorns and green hills vanishing off into the clouds, with here and there a church spire, all beneath a sky bright as bluebells. I could see ancient field systems clearer than I ever had, and to the west, another mound like this one, with people standing on it. Then I realised they weren't people but a stone circle, or trees.

And closer than that, like a mirage, Wylding Hall's towers rose above the greenery, all golden in the sun.

Yet it was impossible that I could see any of this from where we stood. The mound wasn't that high. A wood surrounded it. Beyond that there were more woods that hid the village. I looked for those trees I'd seen, the ring of alders and rowan and hazel.

And yes, there they were, but now they were *below* us: I looked down on a canopy of leaves.

I turned to Julian. "This is crazy."

He laughed. "I know."

"Was there something in that tea you made?"

"Of course not!" He walked to the edge of the mound, the narrow end of the egg, crouched down and stared out across the woods and fields to the hill with the standing stones. "Not that I know of, anyway."

"What is it, then? An optical illusion? A mirage?"

Julian shrugged. "I don't know. I don't care, either. Does it really matter? Isn't it enough that it's all there, and we can see it?"

I should have been more frightened; that came later. It was just too lovely to be scared. Pale green butterflies the size of my thumbnail fed in the bluebells and filled the air like snow. I was afraid I'd step on them, but they seemed to sense where my foot would fall and flew off before it touched the ground. I watched a skylark circle up and up until it disappeared into the blue. Everywhere, little wrens rustled in the grass.

We must have stayed there for an hour. I don't think we spoke another word to each other. Julian remained where he was, staring out into the blue. I walked the perimeter of the mound, then crossed it back and forth. Quartering it. At one point I sat in the grass and searched around, looking for rocks, a flint or coin—the kind of thing you read about people discovering in old burial mounds.

I didn't find anything. I thought of the farmer who'd given me a ride, and wondered if he ever ploughed up ancient coins, or anything else. I'm certain he must have. I wish now I'd gone over to his place and asked him, but of course I would never have dreamed of doing such a thing when I was twenty. Given what they're finding there now at the dig, it might have been useful knowledge.

Finally Julian scrambled back to his feet. He stood for a few more minutes and I could hear him singing under his breath; the same two verses, it sounded like, though I couldn't make out any words. Chanting, almost. I was just learning my craft then, otherwise I might have been more alarmed. Cognisant, at any rate, that he was up to something, and in way over his head.

"We'd better go," he said at last, and turned to me. He looked... different. Calm, but also expectant. "I have a song I want to get down. I want to go over it with Ashton before we begin rehearsing it."

And that was the end of it. He scrambled back down the hill— no holding hands this time, I had to call out to him to wait for me before he raced off into the woods. It was easier going down than up. Julian waited for me at the edge of the copse, looking very impatient.

I turned to gaze back at the mound. It was no higher than it had first appeared. I saw an old oak tree that absolutely towered above it.

"Come on," said Julian.

Without waiting for me, he strode back into the woods. It was only that afternoon, when I went to take a bath, that I found one of those tiny green butterflies had gotten trapped in the folds of my long skirt.

"Look at you," I said, shaking it free, and watched it flutter off into the house.

Ashton

Tom was an incredibly innovative producer. He didn't just manage his bands—he produced their albums as well. He was one of the first who had a mobile recording unit, which meant a band didn't have to go into London to lay down tracks in a studio. The studio could come to you. It was an old delivery lorry that he'd gutted and tricked up with recording decks, tape players and playback machines and amplifiers. It was absolutely state of the art for the time. Richard Branson had one as well—he'd just bought Shipton Manor and was setting up what became the Virgin Records studio. He got the idea for all of that from us and Tom.

Now of course everyone has his own mobile unit, in your laptop or iPhone or whatever. But in those days you were tied to a studio, unless you were fortunate enough to have someone like Tom Haring, who could drive the rig down to Hampshire. And thank God he did, because otherwise there would have been no *Wylding Hall* album, no record whatsoever of what we did that summer.

See, those were never intended to be anything but rough cuts. Tom came down on a lark, he'd just finished kitting out the lorry and he wanted to show it off. Give it a test drive, on the road and with all of us. Course it wasn't on the road much. I think it got about ten miles to the gallon.

I'm not sure who had the idea that we should record outdoors. Jonno? That was the day Billy Thomas was there with his camera, so maybe it was him. Whoever it was, it turned out to be a brilliant idea. We dragged all our instruments out into what used to be the garden. It was all overgrown, flowers everywhere, roses twining up the stone walls and trees covered with wisteria, a carpet of yellow cowslips. Flowers out of season, Lesley said, but they looked wonderful. It all smelled of roses and hashish—Julian broke out his magic box. Grass knee-high and butterflies and grasshoppers dancing through the air. Birds swooping back and forth, and a goshawk circling overhead. It was heaven.

So that's where we set up—in a little English country wilderness. Tom drove the lorry right into the middle of it. Plugged into the house and trailed the electric cords through the grass so we could mike the instruments.

I can't recall how it came about that Billy was there, but however it was, Billy helped with the equipment. We laughed and told him he could sign on as our roadie. I didn't even realise he owned a camera till that afternoon.

Of course the sound quality wasn't anywhere close to what you'd get in a proper studio. But again, we assumed we'd just do that at the end of the summer. This was only for fun, a chance to show off for Tom and give the mobile unit a trial run. You can hear on the album that we were outdoors—the wind in the long grass, bees humming, wrens hopping about. At one point you can hear a plane flying by overhead.

It shouldn't have worked, but it did. It was all live, pretty much a single take. No overdubs. Julian did do an extra take for "Windhover Morn". He was always such a perfectionist.

It was a perfect day, in every way. Weather, happiness. The songs were new and we couldn't get enough of playing them. Tom was flush, he had a hit that summer with "Girl on a String" by the Bullfrogs. One hit wonder, they turned out to be. He rang us that morning and said we weren't to leave, he'd be arriving around noon with a surprise. And so he did, and so it was.

Lesley

That was a magical day. I was having a smoke with Julian when Jonno gave us the news.

"Tom just rang and said he'll be here in a few hours with a surprise. So don't go wandering off, Julian. Keep an eye on him, will you, Les?"

After he went off to tell the others, I turned to Julian. "What do you think the surprise is?"

He shrugged. "Drugs?"

I laughed. There was no way it would be anything like drugs, not with Tom. Never in a million years. He might smoke a bit now and then, and I know he dropped acid at least once, 'cause I was with him. But he was nervous about anything stronger than that, and he was absolutely terrified of any scandal having to do with drugs. There wasn't really a heavy drug scene with folk music, except up in Scotland. Glasgow, that was a tough place. Careers got killed that way—even a few tokes could get you put away in prison for a year. It was still early days for Tom as a producer, and he couldn't afford to lose one of his musicians, especially after the tragedy with Arianna. That was enough scandal to last all of us for a while.

So that was wishful thinking on Julian's part. He had his own little stash of hash, in a little enamelled silver box. A beautiful thing, I have no idea where he got it. About as big as the palm of your hand, it looked like something you'd find in a medieval castle. He kept a block of hash inside and would shave away at it with a penknife. The box's lid was amazing. There was a tree painted on it, in the most remarkable detail—tiny oak leaves, gold and green and yellow, on golden branches no bigger than a blade of grass. The bluest sky you ever saw, peeking through the leaves.

What was most extraordinary was a tiny jewelled bird perched in the tree, no bigger than your pinkie nail. Yet you could see every feather, tiny flecks of emerald and ruby and gold, and a wee little golden beak.

And sapphire eyes—you could only see one eye, its head was cocked, but that eye was a sapphire, I'm sure of it. When it caught the light it winked at you.

It must have been worth a pretty penny, that box. More than any of us earned in a year, all put together. Whenever I asked Julian where it came from, he was always very evasive.

"Someone gave it to me," he said once, but he wouldn't tell me who. "I forgot," he said.

Like you would ever forget whoever gave you a gift like that. Another time he told me he inherited it. I asked his mother once, and she just gave me a blank look.

"A jewelled box? I don't think so. I would have remembered it. Wherever would he have come by something like that?"

Ashton

I remember that box. He kept pills in it. Mandrax, whatever he had. Pot. I looked it up online once. That kind of enamel work, it dates from the 14th century. I always assumed he'd found it at Wylding Hall and nicked it.

We used to joke about discovering treasure, the odd golden mace or grail. Never did, though. We looked once or twice, me and Jonno, got lost wandering through the old wing. There was a passage on the second floor, I think it was a priest-hole. We found it when we pushed aside a wardrobe in one of the bedrooms. I don't think anyone had stepped in that room in two hundred years. We must have walked for ten minutes in the dark—we had a torch but the battery was going. Jonno got spooked and we turned back. I wanted to keep on, but he was dead set against being lost in the dark.

Later, I tried to find that passage again, but I never could. I couldn't remember what room it was. None of them ever looked right.

Jonno

After I told Les and Julian, I found the others. None of us had any idea what Tom had in store, so when Julian pulled out his hash, we all tucked in. Will made breakfast, and we all sat together at that big trestle table in the kitchen and ate. Usually we weren't all up at the same time, so we didn't eat together. But that day we did and it was lovely; everyone laughing and joking, the windows open so the sun came in and warmed the flagstones. I was always barefoot, so I remember that detail.

I also remember when the lorry pulled up. A Ford transit box van, it looked like a milk truck. Tom hopped out, and then this boy. Sturdy lad, dark hair and ruddy face, wearing a work shirt and dungarees.

Well, aren't you nice, I thought. He was a few years younger than me, sixteen. Silas Thomas's grandson. Tom had brought him to help with lugging the sound equipment, which was especially fortuitous when we ended up recording outside. It was fortuitous for me, too, though for a different reason.

Billy Thomas, photographer

Silas Thomas was my grandfather. My family owns the farm next to his. Actually, it's all one farm since he died. I don't live there now, but my partner and I have a cottage not too far off, so we can visit my mum. My father died about ten years ago.

I can't remember exactly when Silas died. I'd left home by then. Maybe five or six years after? Maybe longer. I should remember, I was broke up about it. But I don't.

He told me about the hippies living at Wylding Hall. They hired him to bring them groceries every week. He liked them, as far as I knew. He thought they were harmless. Only thing he worried about was one of them went off into the woods by himself, up to the rath. That's what he called the hill fort. It's an Irish word, his mother was Irish and when she married my great-grandfather and moved here in the 1800s that's what she called it.

So my grandfather said, anyway. He was very superstitious. So was everyone else in the village. None of us was ever supposed to go off playing on our own in the woods, especially not anywhere near the rath. If you did, you'd get a hiding when your folks found out. Julian Blake was the one used to go up there.

The old ways, no one remembers them today. The Wren's a gastropub now, Barry and me quite like it.

I'd heard about the commune in the old manor from my grand-dad. Someone told me they were musicians, a rock group. Of course I'd never seen a rock group. I didn't even have a phonograph. We had a radio, so I'd listen to BBC 3 and John Peel on Saturday nights. That was my connection to the outside world.

I had no thought whatsoever about becoming a rock photographer. I didn't know such a thing existed. I did have a camera, an Instamatic I'd saved for and bought earlier that summer. I was very proud of it. There was a camera club at my secondary school and I wanted to join. So, of course, I needed a camera.

I didn't go to Wylding Hall that day with any thought of snapping photographs. Tom Haring rang up my grandfather and asked if he knew someone who could help carry boxes back and forth from the lorry; cables, things like that. My grandfather volunteered me.

"Make sure you get paid," he said, but I didn't care about that. I was excited to go to Wylding Hall, and to see the hippies.

At the last minute I thought of bringing my camera along. I'd bought a roll of film and loaded it but hadn't taken any pictures yet. I must have thought this would be a good opportunity to take some photographs. It was, and then some.

Tom Haring came by the house and picked me up. He was very nice, very professional. Introduced himself to my mother—my father was out in the field.

Then we drove on to Wylding Hall. He asked me if I'd ever heard of Windhollow Faire. I lied and said yes. I had no idea who they were. We got there and he introduced me around to everyone. Ashton Moorehouse was the only one really looked like a proper rock and roller—he had a beard and long hair and the full hippy regalia, high boots and pirate shirt.

The others had long hair but they seemed normal. Just a few years older than me, very friendly and ordinary. Which was reassuring but a bit of a disappointment. Lesley Stansall, the girl singer, she seemed a bit larger than life; loud voice and always waving her hands around, making a lot of noise. But friendly.

The only one seemed a bit peculiar was Julian Blake. To me he seemed snobbish, though probably he was just stoned.

And I was intimidated by how good-looking he was. I was all mixed up about boys and girls—I was attracted to boys but that was such a horrible thing I couldn't even *think* it. I'd never heard the word "homosexual" and every other word that described it was awful.

So when Julian came shambling into the kitchen and said "Hi" I just mumbled and stared at the floor. The place had a funny smell, like church incense. It wasn't until that night, with Jona-than, that I found out it was hashish. I was such an innocent.

Lesley

I was the one who suggested we record outdoors. It just seemed so obvious to me, although Ashton and Will thought we should do it inside, in the rehearsal room; which was also an obvious choice. I always thought the rehearsal room was the one space that didn't feel like it had a history attached to it. There wasn't this weird sense that we were intruding there, like I got in other parts of Wylding Hall. Whatever history that room had, it was *our* history. We laid it down, made our mark upon the place. I hope it stayed there.

But it was such a gorgeous day, it seemed a shame to be indoors. The garden was in full bloom, such a magical spot that was! Like something out of a book. Old apple trees and blossoming cherry, stock and delphiniums and primroses. Even some narcissus, and they were long out of season. The garden seemed to have its own climate. Things bloomed whenever they wanted, I think. There was a low brick wall around it, very old; the bricks had crumbled so that the back opened out onto the lawn, which was even more overgrown than the garden. Ashton and Will found old-fashioned scythes in one of the outbuildings and they cut away some of the tall grass so we could put our instruments out there, and the microphones. They looked like they'd stepped out of the middle ages. I wish we had photographs of that.

Ashton

It took a few hours to get everything set up in the garden. First we had to hack away at the brush. Then we had to bring in all the cables and power cords, and amplifiers and microphones, all of us tripping over brambles and rosebushes. We dragged out kitchen chairs for us, and the piano stool for Julian. We were all stoned out of our minds, which didn't help matters. But finally it was all done, and we settled down, and played.

I won't go into it again—you have the album. But it was like an enchantment, that one afternoon. We played till the sun was low in the sky but it was still daylight, golden light. Magic hour, film people call it. Tom had brought a teenager from the village, a boy named Billy Thomas. I didn't know he had a camera until he got it from the lorry and came running back through the grass. He shot an entire roll of film, mostly after we'd finished playing and were goofing about, or standing around doing nothing.

Those were the photos that made it onto the album cover and gatefold. He didn't get them developed until autumn, so we didn't see any of them for quite some time. Quite good photos for a kid, I thought. Not what I'd call technically polished, but that's part of their charm, isn't it? The girl, well, I can't account for that. I don't think anyone can.

Billy

I lay there on the grass in the sun and listened while they played. Julian Blake, he offered me a hash pipe, which was the first time I ever smoked. I went into a trance, almost. I wasn't thinking about taking photos. I wasn't thinking about anything, except I liked watching the drummer, Jonathan. He was funny, bit of a clown. I remember he took out two ping pong paddles and started keeping time by slapping them against his thighs. Everyone cracked up, you can hear it if you listen, they didn't edit that out.

Jon didn't seem any older than me. He was short, which might be why I thought he was young. I thought he looked like Michael Palin. He kept peering at me from behind his kit; he wanted to see if I was laughing at his jokes. I was—we all were. When they finished up, it was about four or five in the afternoon. Ashton and Will began tossing around a soccer ball. Don't know where that came from. Lesley went into the house and came out with gallon bottles of cheap wine. Pure rotgut. Julian seemed cheerful; he was quieter than the rest but not what I'd call withdrawn. A bit shy, maybe, but very nice.

I helped Tom Haring roll up the cables back into the lorry, and then he sent me off so I could be with the others. He wanted to check what he'd recorded, make sure everything had worked correctly.

I looked out and saw them cavorting in the garden. It looked like a painting. They all looked very old-fashioned—their clothes were old-fashioned. That was the style. What you see on the album cover, that's how they dressed the entire time they were playing. Lesley in her long peasant dress. Ashton dressed like a pirate. Will looked a bit like my grandfather when he was young, in his wedding photograph. Julian had on a corduroy jacket, stovepipe trousers and Cuban boots, everything well worn.

Jonno was the only one who looked like he was in the right century, jeans and a t-shirt, except that he was wearing a fool's cap with bells on it. I didn't make a big deal that I was taking pictures, but I wasn't secretive. It was just a lark. I wasn't thinking much about it at all. There were twenty frames on that roll, and I'd already taken three of my mum and dad.

About halfway through, a great flock of birds came across the sky. I don't know what kind they were—little birds. But such a crowd of them.that for a moment they blotted out the sun. It was shocking, after all that brilliant sunlight.

That's when everyone turned to look up at the sky, and I snapped that. You can see the manor house in the background, the Elizabethan towers and old chimneys, and the higgledy-piggledy garden with everyone looking up at the sky. On the left-hand side of the frame, you could see the woods that lead to the rath. The first of those pictures was in shadow, because of the birds, but after that they flew off over the trees and the sun shone down again.

It's amazing those photos came out at all. I really had no idea what I was doing.

Jonno

It was evening by the time we'd finished packing up. Tom decided not to drive back to London, so we had an impromptu party. Billy Thomas stayed as well. He and I, we spent the night together. Quite innocently, we both were pissed as newts, with Julian's hash on top of that. And the sheer exhilaration of what we'd done that day! I've never seen Tom that happy, before or since.

Billy and I got to talking, he was a real babe in the woods, very innocent. A true country lad. I asked him up to my room to listen to some albums. He was raving about Lindisfarne and "Fog on the Tyne", which I thought was utter crap. That was the year folk-rock made the charts, Steeleye Span and the rest of them. We all hated that we'd get lumped in with them whenever anyone talked about Windhollow Faire.

I had recently heard about *Transformer* and Tom brought it down from London for me. That's what me and Billy listened to. "Andy's Chest" and "Perfect Day". We started out on the floor but ended up lying side by side in my bed. I kissed him and we snogged, but that was all. Fell asleep that way.

When I woke up in the morning, he wasn't there—he'd caught a ride back to the village with Tom. In the autumn, I saw the photographs he'd taken, but I didn't see Billy again for about ten years. We're good mates now.

Tom

I thought we had accomplished something breathtaking with that session, and I believed it was a harbinger of great things to come. The beginning of something wonderful for Windhollow Faire, when in fact it was the opposite.

Will

About a week after we laid down those rough cuts in the garden, we all decided to go down to the pub and have another go at busking. Julian wasn't crazy about the idea, but I reminded him we'd been practicing "Lost Tuesdays" all week and this would be a good place to debut it for an audience other than ourselves. We'd run out of booze, too.

It was Saturday, a rainy day; might have been the only time it rained that whole summer. I think it actually was. We'd been on our own all week, Tom was long gone and we'd decided not to invite anyone else down. We just wanted to focus on the music.

You forget now, how strange and original those songs were for their time. When you got tagged as a folk band, especially a trad band like we were, supposedly—well, you were supposed to play traditional songs, weren't you, acoustic guitar and all the rest, and traditional arrangements.

We weren't having any of that. Especially me. I'd made an electric fiddle, hooking my own up to the innards of an old Hoover. Julian had written "Darkling Sea" for him and Ashton to play on acoustic guitar and upright bass, but I bulled my way into it, as is my wont. Les and Julian had worked out these gorgeous harm-onies, you'd hear them singing first thing in the morning and last thing at night.

Something had happened between them, I never figured out what. I thought maybe Nancy and Julian had gone off together during the notorious non-orgy, but that doesn't seem to have been the case. Hard to imagine the two of them in a passionate embrace, but stranger things have happened.

Whatever it was, there was still a bit of a chill between Lesley and Julian. Odd thing was, their singing was brilliant. You learn to do that if you're in a band—put aside whatever it is comes between you the rest of the time. Sex, drink, politics, marriage, whatever it is. If you can't do that, well that's when it all falls apart.

Jon

I drove the van that night. I wanted to keep a clear head, which is why I'm the one whose account you should trust. We'd all been boozing it up pretty steadily, Les and Will especially. Me and Julian mostly just smoked, though that week I finished an entire bottle of Jameson's all by myself. Ashton kept to beer most of the time. I always wondered if he found some way to secretly pop down to The Wren. Probably he did.

Something changed after that weekend when Will's girlfriend Nancy came to visit. I don't think it had anything to do with her. It was like the dynamic within the group shifted into some stranger, higher gear. Emphasis on "higher".

No, not really. But there was that one night when we all lay around in the dark and felt—something. I think it only happens when you're young. This weird sense of possibility; a kind of knowledge. You know there's a door, and even if you can't see it, you can sense it opening, and if you're quick enough, you can slip inside.

Will and Les and I used to talk about it. Ashton thought it was all bollocks, but me and Will and Les, we thought, you know, maybe it could happen. Maybe it did.

It didn't take too much to convince Julian to come down to the pub. He was shy, but he wasn't that shy about performing. He was self-conscious. Will or Ashton are good at banter, and Lesley, she'll trip over her own feet and make a joke of it. The audience loved her.

Julian wasn't like that, but he didn't freeze up in front of a crowd. I know that's the accepted wisdom, but it's wrong. He was more like me. I get behind my kit and hide there. Unless you're Keith Moon or John Bonham, no one's looking at the drummer.

Once he got settled, Julian would just focus on his singing and his guitar. He had incredible powers of concentration—the whole time we were at Wylding Hall, if he wasn't playing with the rest of us downstairs, he was up in his room, studying transcendental meditation or some mystic shite.

Only with him it wasn't really shite—he really could go into kind of a trance when he played. We've all been there, catching a groove, but this was different. Uncanny. To be honest, I wasn't sure how it'd go over at the pub.

Lesley

I have no clue what went on between Julian and Nancy, but something did. I know that. He was different after that weekend, not just different towards me but...changed, somehow. Back then you'd meet people who got involved with cults. Jesus freaks or swami so-and-so. Julian never joined a cult that I knew of, but he had that same glittery look in the eye, like he'd seen something amazing but was going to keep it secret because, you know, the rest of us weren't worthy.

Nancy wasn't exactly like that, but she was a self-professed witch. And she does have a gift. She sees things others can't. I don't think she's making it up, either. She may be slightly deluded, but she's not lying. That weekend she stayed with us, I think she inadvertently encouraged Julian in whatever fixation he'd developed.

Wylding Hall didn't help, either. The whole time we were there, it was like being in a dream. Everything conspired to keep us from waking up. The weather and drugs and alcohol, the occult talk and crazy books and sexual tensions.

And that house—you could just get lost in it. Whenever I explored the old Tudor wing by myself, I'd find locked doors that wouldn't open; then the next time, they would. No one had a key. One of the rooms had been a ballroom—shredded tapestries on the walls, floor covered with dust. Overlooking it was a minstrel gallery with an amazing oak screen, carved with all kinds of strange things. Birds with human faces. People with wings like dragonflies or wasps.

I used to stare up at the minstrel gallery, but no matter how hard I looked, I could never find the way in. No stairs, no ladder. There must've been a secret passage somewhere, but I never found it.

Jon

There were maybe forty people at the pub that night. Will said he counted thirty-seven, but I think he left out the barman. Call it forty. That pub was tiny, so it felt more crowded, but it wasn't what you'd call standing room only. It was Saturday night, all the regulars were there—I guess they were regulars, I didn't know them from Adam. The barman was a good bloke, he said we could set up and play in a corner.

We went acoustic—none of us wanted to lug amps and electric guitars and a PA. I just had my tambour and some shakers and an African drum a friend brought back from Tangiers. Very low-tech.

What did they think? Folks at the pub seemed more bemused than anything else when we walked in. They certainly weren't hostile. The barman had a thing for Les, which made it easier—we knew we wouldn't get tossed out. So we set up, tuned up, and away we went. They loved it.

Ashton

To be honest, I was quite nervous for the first few songs. It wasn't like when me and Les played on our own that time—there were a lot more people, for one. And it felt somehow like we were there to make a statement. Territorial, almost. We were interlopers, remember, longhaired hippy outsiders at a time when there was a lot of hostility toward that kind of person.

I could hear some muttering while we were tuning up—who the feck were we, gipsies squatting in the old manor and prancing about the forests, etcetera. Someone must have seen Julian stargazing in the woods. For some reason that got them especially worked up.

Still, once we started playing, everyone got quieter. We started with "John Barleycorn", a traditional folk song; we thought that might lull them into a false sense of security. But after that we did our own stuff. Lesley's new songs—we kicked off with "Cloud Prince", thought it would be good to put the girl singer out front.

Lesley—they loved her. A few of them tried taking the piss because of her accent. She might have been the first American some of them had seen since the war. But she only flung her long hair about and laughed and bantered with them. No mike, but she didn't need one—her voice filled that place like nothing you ever heard. They just ate it up. Kept passing her pints while she was singing.

We did four or five songs, then took a break. Les passed the hat, the barman bought us a round then we bought his. When we came back, it was Julian's turn.

Jon

Second set, there were a few more people. No one had mobile phones back then, so you couldn't text your friends and say rush down to The Wren to hear history in the making. But a few of the younger blokes left and came back with their wives or girlfriends.

We pulled up a chair for Julian. Lesley had stood, she always liked moving around. But Julian liked to sit, so I grabbed him a chair.

He cut quite a figure, he was so tall, and a bit of a dandy. Always the same old brown corduroy jacket, but it looked very sharp. The sleeves were a bit short, but I think he might have kept it on purpose, so people would focus on his hands when he played.

He had such big hands—big bony wrists, extraordinarily long fingers. That's why he was such an incredible guitarist—his reach was terrific. He had very eccentric tunings, which meant you could never duplicate how he played—and believe me, people tried. Jimmy Page told me once he listened to *Wylding Hall* a hundred times, trying to figure out Julian's fingering on "Windhover Morn". He couldn't.

Still, The Wren wasn't exactly the venue to impress people with your eccentric tunings. Only, of course, Julian did.

Tom

Over the years, I can't tell you how many people have told me they saw that gig. All total bullshit, of course. No one saw it, except for a few dozen people who lived in that village. I suspect a lot of them are dead now. Maybe the younger ones are telling their kids and grandkids, "yeah, I was there when Windhollow Faire first played the songs from *Wylding Hall*." I guess that's possible.

But if I had a pound for every person told me they were at The Wren that night, I wouldn't be living here in Sheffield, I'll tell you that.

Will

Now, you have to picture Julian, this tall figure sitting in a battered pub chair: hunched over his guitar, long brown hair fall-ing over his face.

"That a girl?" some geezer called out, and the punters all laughed.

But Julian just kept tuning his guitar. A string broke and for a moment I thought he'd lost it—that he'd just slink off somewhere and give it up.

He didn't. I tell you, I can see it in my mind's eye like it happened last night, those big hands and that wristwatch he loved so much. He looked at his watch then glanced around the pub, like he was searching for someone. I remember thinking "Who the hell's he looking for?" He didn't know anyone around there, as far as I knew.

People were getting impatient. *We* were getting impatient. Me and Les exchanged a look, she was wondering if maybe she should just take charge and start singing.

Then Julian began to play. "Windhover Morn", "Cloud Prince". For the third or fourth song, he did "Thrice Tosse These Oaken Ashtes". People know the song now because of *Wylding Hall*, but no one knew it then. It's based on a seventeenth century air by Thomas Campion. I'd come across it at Cecil Sharp House earlier that year but decided not to use it. Les called me on that much later, said I'd been superstitious. Perhaps I was.

The peculiar thing is that Julian had come across it as well, only he found it in the library at Wylding Hall. I didn't even know there *was* a library there until he told me. He discovered it in some old book, and he said his version was far older than Campion's, and with slightly different words. When we'd recorded it in the garden, Julian went with the original.

But that night at The Wren, he sang the older version. He'd composed new music for it, a very eerie melody. Unfortunately we never recorded that version of the song. We all remember him singing it, but none of us has ever been able to recreate Julian's music. Believe me, we tried.

As soon as he opened his mouth and began to sing, the room fell quiet. Not just quiet: dead silent. I've never seen anything like it. Like a freeze-frame in a movie. Nobody spoke, nobody moved. Nobody *breathed*. I know I didn't, not for half a minute. It sounded as though he were whispering the song into your ear.

That night at The Wren, you could see that's how every single person felt. Like he was singing to each one of them, alone, just his voice and those few chords over and over again. Once he finished his version, he went into the more familiar one.

Thrice tosse these Oaken ashes in the ayre;
Thrice sit though mute in this inchained chayre:
And thrice three times tye up this true loves knot,
And come soft shee will, or shee will not.

Lesley

It was the first time he performed the Campion song. I'd heard him practicing bits of it in his room, but he never sang it for us when we were rehearsing. I recognised the tune immediately. It was the same one I'd heard the night that Nancy was there. The song we'd all heard, only none of us could replicate it afterward, or even remember it.

It was like someone dragged a razor across my skin—not enough to draw blood, just a cold blade drawn down my neck, never enough to break the skin. I almost cried out—I would have, but my voice was gone. I know it sounds crazy, but I felt as though my own voice had been sucked into his, my breath. My heart beating at the same time as his. Nothing but that song and that voice, and his guitar. None of us have ever been able to play that song since.

Jon

He'd just finished playing the bridge when I saw her. She was in the corner, watching him. I didn't see her walk in.

At first I thought she was a young boy; very slim and fine-boned, white-blonde hair. A real towhead. She was so pale I mistook her for light reflecting on the mirror behind her. Took a minute for my eyes to focus and see it was a girl.

I'd put her at fifteen, sixteen. She looked younger because she was so thin, but when you got a better look, her face wasn't young. Not old, just—she looked like she knew things. Her skin was the whitest skin I've ever seen—you could see where the veins were. It made her skin greenish, like a luna moth's. She was wearing a long floaty white dress, ragged at the hem. Barefoot, leaves stuck to her feet like she'd been walking in the woods.

I didn't think she was that unusual—you couldn't throw a rock in the King's Road and not hit some Pre-Raphaelite teenybopper. Pale and interesting. Still, I suspect it raised a few eyebrows with the punters in The Wren.

But with her it wasn't makeup. I saw that when she walked over, after the set. She was the palest creature I'd ever set eyes on. I couldn't take my eyes off her, same way I felt about Julian. When the two of them stood beside each other, you didn't know where to look.

Patricia

There's an old West Country ballad called "The Lady of Zennor". Will turned me onto it when I interviewed him for that long piece I did for *Mojo* about Windhollow's legacy. It's based on a legend about a mermaid. Zennor's a fishing village in Cornwall. I visited it after talking to Will, he told me there was a memorial in the village church. I thought he was having me on, but damned if it wasn't the truth.

The story goes that there was a young man in the village who sang in the church choir. His voice was so beautiful that every Sunday a mermaid would come out of the sea and walk up to the church and sit in the back just to hear him. I don't know how she walked with a tail—they didn't go into that. Eventually she converted to Christianity so she could marry him. The church is ancient, twelfth century, and when you go inside you can see where she sat—someone made a special little wooden pew for her, with a mermaid carved on each end. I sat in it—no one was there to stop me. The church was empty and I could have walked out with it if I wanted, it was so small. She must have been tiny.

I asked Will why he was telling me about this particular legend and song. Obviously I knew why, but I wanted to hear him say it, even if it was off the record. He wouldn't.

Lesley

No, I didn't like her, not that I had time to get to know her. I didn't trust her. I knew too many male singers, and you didn't have to be Jimmy Page to get a bunch of fourteen-year-old girls hopping into bed with you.

I also knew that Tom Haring would pitch a fit when he found out. Which he did. The whole point of us being at Wylding Hall was to avoid distractions, and groupies are definitely a distraction. God knows how she knew we were there. Someone must have heard about Ashton and me singing at the pub, and blabbed it around.

She certainly wasn't from the village—every guy in that place just about keeled over when he saw her, even Jonno.

And yes, of course I was jealous. Anyone would have been. She was like some hippy wet dream, platinum blonde in that slinky white dress. Not even a dress—it was a white slip, it might have been a hundred years old. It was sheer enough you could see she wasn't wearing any underwear.

This is all we need, I thought, to get run out of town because some naked teenager shows up at the pub.

But Jonno, God bless him, he had the sense to give her his cape to cover up. And yes, he did wear a cape, a long sky-blue velvet cape that cost a fortune. It looked a lot better on her. What the hell's a drummer going to do with a freaking cape? Jonno threw it over her and pulled her over to our table. Which, fortunately, was in the back corner. They all just fawned around her like she was the Queen or some such shit—Will and Ashton and Jonno.

And Julian, of course. Soon as he finished that song he jumped up, grabbed his guitar and—I swear, I never saw him move so fast. He raced over and grabbed her hand, and just stared down at her.

My first thought was they knew each other, like she was an old girlfriend, or someone from school. Yet he wasn't looking at this girl like he knew her. It was more like he was totally amazed. For a second I even thought she was someone from the press or maybe a rock star, some bigwig he'd invited but hadn't imagined would really show up.

But it immediately became obvious she wasn't. I can't describe it, but she gave off this weird vibe. You know how you'll see a crazy person in the street, and even though they're not acting overtly crazy—like, they're talking to themselves, so maybe they're on a mobile phone. But you just know there's no mobile phone. You just know, that person is nuts.

That's how I felt about her. Like maybe she was on drugs and might pull a knife, or God knows what. She looked strung out; didn't know where she was, didn't know her name. Ashton kept asking her, *who are you, who are you?* until Julian told him to shut the fuck up.

That alone was enough of a warning. Julian never lost his temper. Ever.

Whoever she was, I didn't want her anywhere near me.

Ashton

Well, I thought, where's Julian been hiding *this?* Still waters run deep! Here's this drop-dead gorgeous wisp of a girl comes running up to him. I couldn't believe my eyes.

Also, she was just about starkers. When Jonno wrapped his idiotic cape around her, I wanted to throttle him—doesn't hurt to look! But I suppose it was for the best.

Clearly she and Julian knew each other. They clung together like kids, you couldn't have slid a penny between them. After about five minutes it got to be a bit much.

"All right," I said. "Time, gentlemen, time."

I put my hand on Julian's shoulder, and he jumped like I'd given him an electric shock.

"What did you say?" he demanded. He had actually gone white.

"Just a joke," I said. I looked over and saw good old Les had been the first to do something sensible. "Look, here's Les with a round, let's drink up and head back home, what do you think?"

Julian took the girl by the hand. "She's coming with me."

"Of course she is." I handed him a pint. Lesley had only brought five, I noted.

"We didn't get much money," she said. She looked angry. "I had to buy a round for Reg."

Just as well, the wee girl didn't seem like she'd be able to handle her drink. Seemed a bit stunned, deer in the headlamps.

I glanced around to see if anyone in the pub recognised her. She might have been someone's kid. *That* wouldn't go over well—rock and rollers coming in to kidnap their women and children.

But no one seemed to know her. If anything, they seemed to be making a point of *not* looking at her. Because of how she was dressed, I thought at the time. Or undressed. There were bits of stuff stuck to her feet. Dead leaves, I thought, but when I looked closer—and I wanted to look closer, believe me—it wasn't leaves, but feathers.

That's weird, I thought; someone's been in the henhouse.

I assumed she was some local character—you know, local halfwit or drug casualty, a poor thing everyone recognised but never spoke about. Not to her face, anyway. That's why I thought only a couple of quid got tossed in the hat.

It wasn't because of Julian's set, I'll tell you that. He was magnificent. Even the punters were impressed; I heard them talking once they found their voices. They'd never heard the like. *I'd* never heard the like, and I saw Jimi Hendrix at an afterhours once with Jeff Beck and Sandy Denny. That night, Julian fucking blew them out of the water.

Tom

Unsurprisingly, Lesley was the one blew the whistle on that gig. Very early Monday morning I got a phone call from her. Way too early for an ordinary phone call, not that I received many of those from anyone in Windhollow. I thought they'd run out of money again.

But that wasn't why she rang. She gave me the rundown, said this strange girl had shown up two nights earlier at a pub gig and disappeared with Julian into his room. The two of them hadn't been seen since.

Let me tell you, I wasn't happy about Windhollow busking at the pub. But what's done is done. As for Julian taking up with some little teenybopper, who cares? I certainly didn't.

"Well, I just thought you should know," said Lesley. I could hear her pouring something into a glass, she was hitting it pretty hard back then. "I haven't seen him since Saturday night. Her either."

"It doesn't sound like we need to call Scotland Yard, Les. He's needed a good lay since Arianna died. Go easy on him."

I'd had no idea Lesley and Julian had been sleeping together, otherwise I wouldn't have been so blunt. By the long silence that followed, I realised they must have been involved. Fuck, I thought, now Les will fall to pieces.

She didn't, though. "My room's next to theirs and I haven't heard a peep," she said. "They could be lying dead in there for all we know. That girl—I think she's unstable."

Now I did start to get anxious. Also angry. There'd been rumours of Julian and drugs but I'd tried to ignore them. This sounded like it might be something more serious, like maybe the girl had brought something with her—heroin or cocaine. Hard drugs.

"For Christ's sakes, Les, why are you ringing me in London? Get Jonno and Ashton to break the door down! Or ring the police. No, wait—"

All I needed was some kind of Redlands drug scandal with musicians and a naked girl. Or an OD.

Or—and I feel guilty even saying this—something worse. Because Julian was the one who'd always struck me as unstable. Not dangerous, but tightly corked, the way upper-middle-class English guys could be.

Arianna's suicide flashed before me. We only had Julian's word that she had jumped to her death. There'd been an inquest but no investigation. Julian's father was well-placed and had some connections, and the whole tragic event had been dispensed with very quickly.

It hadn't crossed my mind before, and God forgive me for saying it now. But at that moment I thought that perhaps Julian had killed Arianna. And now he'd killed this second girl.

"No, don't do anything with the police," I quickly told Lesley. "I'm coming up there, I'll be as fast as I can. Just hold tight."

I don't know what I imagined I might do if it turned out that Julian really had killed someone. Spirit Les out of the country, at least. She was so young and an American to boot. I could just see the headlines: Innocent Yank seduced by decadent rockers, dead teenager in the room next door...

Of course, in the long term, you can't buy that kind of publicity.

Lesley

I got off the phone with Tom and I was shaking. Booze was part of it—I needed a couple of drinks before I got up the nerve to call him, especially that early on a Monday morning.

Still, it was more than drink made me shake. I *was* jealous, but I was even more frightened. There was something deeply unsettling about that girl. The way she looked and appeared out of nowhere; the way Julian reacted when he first saw her.

But also the way she stuck in my mind—like a song you can't get out of your head. An earworm. She was like a brain-worm. No matter how hard I tried not to think about her, I kept seeing that little white face and hair and those spooky eyes.

That's what creeped me out the most—her eyes were so pale you couldn't see what colour they were. Not blue and not green, though you'd see flickers of those. Not grey, either. They were like water— they took on whatever colour was around them. She'd flick her tongue out to lick her lips over and over, little bit of a tongue like a cat's. Or a snake's. There was something wrong about her, something horrible.

I was afraid to go into Julian's room by myself, but I couldn't bring myself to wake up anyone else. It was only six a.m., they'd be furious.

And what was I going to say? "I'm worried because Julian's been in there with that girl since Saturday night." They'd just laugh at me.

So I went alone. For a long time I stood in front of the door, listening. It was a very still morning, not a breath of wind. Sun shining but I didn't hear a bird outside and that seemed odd, too. You'd always hear birds at first light, they'd make such a racket you couldn't fall back asleep. But that morning, nothing.

I don't know how long I stood there. Ten minutes at least. Maybe longer. I was thinking maybe I'd go back for another splash of vodka, when I heard a noise from inside Julian's room. Something soft struck the wall, just once. Not like someone knocking, more like something had been thrown. A kind of muffled sound, like whatever it was had been wrapped in cloth or newspaper.

I held my breath and listened for voices or someone moving around inside, but everything had gone silent. I was starting to think maybe I'd imagined it, when the sound came again, much louder this time.

Whatever it was had been thrown against the door in front of me. I jumped backward, and heard it again.

Whump. Whump. Whump.

After a minute the sound stopped. I crept back to the door, and it started up again. Now the noise came from the other end of the room, by the window. I pressed my ear against the door and listened.

"Julian?" I whispered. Then louder, "Julian?"

I took a deep breath, put my hand on the knob, cracked the door open and peered inside. I saw nothing but the usual mess—clothes and books on the floor.

"Julian?"

No answer. I went inside, the door closing behind me.

The room was empty, the bed was empty. I can't tell you what would have been worse, to see Julian dead or to see him in bed with that girl. But there was no one at all.

I stepped over a pile of books and saw Julian's guitar leaning against the bed, as though he'd been playing it. The clothes he'd been wearing at the pub were on the floor. So was Jonno's blue cape. The window was cracked open two or three inches. Everything was utterly still. The bed sheets were tossed around—it was obvious no one could be hiding there, but still I pulled back the coverlet.

Immediately I wished I hadn't. There was blood on the bottom sheet—not much, just a few large drops, dried now. I yanked the coverlet back. I looked under the pillows—don't ask me what I was looking for. I even rested my hand on the mattress, testing to see if it was warm.

Of course it wasn't. Finally I turned to look at the wall.

At first I thought Julian had scribbled there. It was covered in little dark jots and blots, like musical notes. The walls in our bedrooms were white plaster, and Will liked to write on his, ideas for songs, phone numbers, girl's names.

But these marks weren't ink or pencil. They were tiny dots of fresh blood, speckled across the plaster like someone had flicked a paint brush at it.

The other wall was the same—and the ceiling, and the back of the door. Blood was spattered everywhere, not great splashes of it but droplets, no bigger than a pinprick. My heart started pounding. I wanted to run for the door but my legs were like jelly.

And then I heard it again, this time behind me—that same soft *whump*. My mouth was so dry that when I tried to scream nothing came out. I turned.

A tiny dark blur hovered just outside the window, like a leaf blowing against the glass. Another *whump*, and the dark blur fell to the windowsill inside the room. A tiny bird, motionless.

Now I could move, and I did, very cautiously. The window glass was like the walls, spattered with blood. The dead bird lay on the sill. It would barely have filled my palm. Its feathers were reddish-brown, white at the breast. The wingtips were darker, almost black. Each toothpick leg had long, reddish claws. Eyes like poppy seeds. Its tiny beak wasn't quite shut, and it was leaking blood. I leaned down and softly blew on it, but it didn't stir.

I found a sheet of paper on the floor. I slid it beneath the dead bird, then slid the bird into my palm.

It didn't weigh a thing. The feathers were so soft I could scarcely feel them. But when I drew it to my face to get a closer look, the tiny body shifted, and one of its claws pierced my palm.

It was like I'd been pricked by a hot needle. I yelped and dropped the bird back onto the windowsill, then stepped back and waited to see if the bird would move. Maybe it was playing dead.

Finally I gave up and left. It wasn't until I took a bath that evening that I saw the skin where its claw had pricked me was swollen, like I'd gotten a splinter. It hurt like hell, so badly I couldn't play guitar for a week.

Then it burst, like a boil. Eventually it healed, but it left a scar. It still aches sometimes when I play.

Jon

Monday after we played the pub, Tom comes barrelling back up to Wylding Hall in his car. I thought someone had died, he was driving so fast. Les had called him with some mad story about Julian and a girl and Tom was shouting "Are they dead? Are they dead?"

I had no idea what he was on about—why would they be dead? He stormed into the house, shouting and running upstairs then down again. We're all in the kitchen. Les had woken us up, raving on about Julian but she didn't tell us she'd rang Tom. Tom grabbed Ashton first.

"Where's Julian?"

Ashton looked at Tom like he was raving mad. "Julian? How the hell would I know? Did you look in his room?"

"He's not there."

"He probably took a walk then." Now Ashton is the one with his knickers in a twist. "What's this about? Why aren't you in London?"

So it comes out that Les had rung up Tom at the crack of dawn, woke him and told him Julian had gone missing with a girl from the pub. Ashton just about exploded—he did *not* like being woken up out of a sound sleep, even at the best of times. He started yelling at Les.

"Are you mad? Why'd you ring Tom? Because Julian took off with some bird? I would too, if I had you dogging me all the time."

"And me," agreed Will. "You're acting like a mad cow, Les."

I didn't weigh in—I felt sorry for Les. And I'm an early riser, so I was already up.

Well, you can imagine what happened next. Lesley fell apart, sobbing and wailing about what a bunch of bastards we all were, how Tom was the only one who cared about what happened to her or the band and now even he had given up.

"Don't be an idiot," Tom snapped. "If I didn't care, d'you think I'd be here? Christ. Is there any tea?"

"In a flash," I said.

I made another pot of tea and some toasted cheese sandwiches. I wanted to get out of that room fast; but I knew that everyone would feel better once they got a bit of food in them.

Ashton

Jonno was the one saved the day that time. He was always looking out for everyone—you know, "Cuppa tea, mate?" or sharing his fags if you ran out. In he comes with tea and a tray of sandwiches and a couple of reefers, and we all eat and smoke a bit of weed and everyone starts to feel better. Except for Les, who went up to her room and refused to come down.

Truth is, often Lesley got the fuzzy end of the lollypop. Didn't get enough credit for the songs she wrote or the arrangements she came up with, didn't get credit for how much of our live performances she carried. Especially when Julian was around. He overshadowed everyone.

Later, she was the one became a big star. The rest of us might have been forgotten, if it wasn't for *Wylding Hall*. But we never took Lesley seriously enough.

And we absolutely didn't take her seriously that morning. I mean, who would have? She was going on about birds flying around inside the house and someone bashing at the walls and Julian being murdered in his bed by that little groupie he'd picked up. But Tom had checked out his room and didn't see anything strange. After a while me and Jonno and Will went up, and Julian was gone; Lesley was dead right about that. But we didn't find anything else.

Will

I just assumed Julian had taken off with the girl. Not for good, just for a stroll in the woods or down to the village. His car hadn't moved. His room was empty. The bed looked like it'd been slept in. None of us was playing detective, it's not like we searched for fingerprints or anything like that.

Ashton poked around under the bed, nothing there but old socks and scribbled notes for songs. There were books scattered everywhere, and Jonno started going through them. He was the one thinking most like a police detective. He found a couple of letters from Lesley, love letters, and a letter from Julian's mum and dad back in Hampstead.

But nothing that might have belonged to the girl, and nothing like a note from Julian saying that he'd gone away. It all looked like he'd just stepped out for a smoke or a walk, the way he did most every morning.

Finally Ashton threw a pillow at me. "This is a total waste of time," he said. "He'll be back for lunch, though if he's smart about it he won't bring the girl." But he never came back.

Tom

I got there around noon. Everyone was in the kitchen, and they all looked out of sorts. *I* was out of sorts. There was a blow-up because Lesley had called me—they never liked me coming down to check on them, and they thought I'd be angry that they'd played a gig at the pub without telling me. I was more concerned that something had happened to Julian. One of the boys said something to Lesley, I don't remember what, but she flew off in tears. I thought it was best to leave her alone until I could figure out what the hell was going on. There was no sign of Julian, but so what?

"What about this girl, then?" I asked them.

All of a sudden everyone is very quiet. *So that's the problem*, I thought.

No one wants to tell me about her, and when finally Jonno pipes up, all I get is that a young girl had shown up at the pub and come back with Julian.

"Who is she?"

Jonno shrugged. "I have no idea."

Neither did anyone else.

"What's her name then?" I asked.

Again, nothing. I was exasperated, but I still wasn't concerned. Pretty girl shows up, goes home with a musician—where's the news in that? I was cheesed off about the pub gig, and I reamed them out about that, and then it was over.

Or so I thought.

I didn't hang around. It was Monday, I'd postponed a meeting with some session musicians and I needed to get back to London. I had a cup of tea and told them to let me know when Julian returned and to make their peace with Lesley. I told them I'd make room in the calendar for them to come into the studio in two weeks.

It was mid-August by then, and the lease on Wylding Hall only ran to the end of the month. Everything had seemed fine when I'd brought the mobile unit down just a few weeks earlier. Now I was worried that maybe things weren't so rosy. I wanted to record the album before anyone got ideas about leaving the group.

On the way out to my car I peeked into Julian's Morris Minor, to see if maybe he'd spent the night there. But it looked exactly as it had when he first arrived at the beginning of the summer.

Ashton

Of course I blame myself. We all did, and still do. But you never expect something like this to happen, for someone to suddenly disappear without a trace. Every day I thought he'd show up again. When a week went by and he hadn't, I assumed he'd taken off with the girl.

I was furious: fucking Julian had scuttled everything. We couldn't do the studio album without him. That was never on the table—it was inconceivable, then or now, that we could have done *Wylding Hall* without Julian. His guitar, his voice; all the songs he'd written.

And I am not downplaying Lesley's contribution. She and Julian, their harmonies on "Windhover Morn" were exquisite. And she wrote three of the songs. But any one of us might have been replaced in the studio. Julian? Never.

Will

That Wednesday or Thursday I went down to the pub to ask the barman if he'd seen Julian. He had not. I asked about the girl, if she was a local girl from the village. He said he'd never seen her before but that she might have been someone's daughter, he just didn't know. There were a couple of geezers at the bar, but when I asked them about the girl, I got the fish-eye. One of them said something like, "That's what you get hunting birds out of season". I assumed he meant the girl was underage.

That freaked me out—I thought maybe the town elders had lynched Julian for going off with one of their kids. And that very well may be what happened. I didn't stick around the pub after that.

Ashton

Will told us he thought one of the locals might have done something to Julian. That was the first time I thought that maybe this wasn't going to end well.

Lesley

I waited a week then rang the police. I will never forgive myself for not going to them sooner. But I was so angry at Will and Ashton and Jonno, especially Ashton, and I didn't want to do anything that would give them any cause whatsoever to call me a hysterical female.

And I was angry at Julian, too—enraged and heartbroken. And that girl. If I had seen her, I would have throttled her.

The police did nothing. The sergeant actually laughed when I spoke to him on the telephone.

"Eh wot, love? You want us to mount a search for your boyfriend? Maybe you should search for another bloke!"

The next day I made Jonno drive me to the police station. We went in and tried to file a missing persons report, but the police wouldn't let us. In retrospect we should have gotten dressed up—we looked like what we were, a couple of scruffy hippies. There was no way they were going to take us seriously.

When we got back to Wylding Hall I told Will I thought he should call Julian's parents—he knew them. He said if he did they'd freak out and he didn't want to worry them for no reason. I told him it looked like there was definitely a reason. But he didn't do it.

That's when I rang up Tom again and told him that Julian still hadn't returned, and I thought he should call Julian's parents. He said he would, and he did, but he waited another week. By then it was too late.

Tom

It's true, I did wait. I know how bad that sounds, but I saw no point in having them worry needlessly. Kids were always taking off back then, hitchhiking to Katmandu to find themselves. Julian told me once he wanted to visit Morocco, to see what a different, more ancient culture was like. It would have been absolutely in character for him to do something like that without telling the rest of us, especially if there was a woman involved.

But I finally did ring them up. It went as you would expect. Julian's father was very stiff-upper-lip, not unconcerned but he thought that Julian very likely had decided to take a trip someplace. He was less sanguine about the girl. They were conservative people, Julian's mum and dad, wait-for-marriage types.

His mother didn't fall apart, but I could hear from her voice that she was distressed, especially when I told her that Julian's car was still at Wylding Hall.

"Why wouldn't he have taken the car?" she asked. "It makes no sense to me, that he wouldn't have taken the car."

Next morning they called the police.

Lesley

The police did fuck-all to find Julian. They listened to his parents, and I'm sure they were more polite to them than to us, but they just kept saying he'd most likely gone off with some girl and one day they'd show up back home with a grandbaby in tow.

Eventually they did file it as a proper missing person's case. I don't know how long it was before they did that—several months at least. You could find out by checking the police department in Canterbury, if they keep records that far back. If they keep records at all. Fuckwits.

We were all back in London by then. Jonno was in touch with Billy Thomas, and Billy said there had been cops out to Wylding Hall. They questioned him and his grandfather—poor Silas! I asked if they'd questioned the men at the pub, but Jonno didn't know.

They questioned us, eventually. Especially me. God's own irony there: I was the only one thought he'd met with foul play, and I end up being the one they suspect of it. Course they didn't find anything at all, with me or anyone else.

I think his parents kept hoping he'd come back. I don't know if they ever had him declared dead or whatever it is you do. I mean, what would anyone do? It's such a horrible thing, never knowing.

They're both dead now, some years ago. He was their only child. They took great pride in the album, I know that. I only met them that once, when it was released and Tom had a party at the Moonthunder office. They were very nice, very normal, upper middle-class. That was in October; he'd only been gone two months and we all still thought he'd be back. It was too awful to think anything else.

Jon

I really did think he'd come back. I still do—I know, it's crazy, but I do. He always wanted to go to Morocco, we talked about that a lot. He had that album Brian Jones did before he died, *The Pipes of Pan in Joujouka*—mad old Arab men in the desert, playing flutes and drums. Ancient-sounding music. Julian and I used to get stoned and listen to it in my room. No one else could stand it, but Julian loved it. It sounded like music from the dawn of time, like what you'd get if you set a time machine for the Dark Ages.

To me, it seems entirely possible that he ran off to Morocco or Tangier and decided to stay there, like Paul Bowles or William Burroughs. Smoke hash all day, hang around the souk, play the oud. Julian would love that.

Ashton

That girl—there was something disturbed me about that girl. I'm with Lesley on that one.

Years later, Tricia Kenyon told me she'd seen a ghost at Wylding Hall, that time she came down and interviewed us. She described it to me and I said, "Good Christ, you saw the girl!" She said that's why she'd finally told me. When I asked her why she hadn't said anything sooner, she just shook her head.

"No one would have believed me," she said. "And besides, what difference would it have made?"

And you know, she was right on both counts.

Will

When Julian left, that was the beginning of the end. We didn't know it right away—we kept thinking he'd reappear, and things would go back to the way they were.

But everything changed after that. It wasn't just that we missed him, although we did. We *needed* him. Without Julian, there was no Windhollow Faire. There would be no second album. None of us was thinking he was gone for good, but we knew we couldn't record the album without him.

But we couldn't afford to wait. Tom had been talking us up back in London. Patricia Kenyon had written that piece for *NME* and they were eager to run it—they didn't want to wait till the album was released. Tom was tearing his hair out, he'd booked studio time for us, and even though it was his studio, time is money. He wanted the new album to be out by the end of the year, so it would get a boost from Christmas shoppers.

None of us had gotten any kind of advance for a second album. Tom was out of pocket for the lease on Wylding Hall, and all of our other expenses as well. We were all totally, utterly skint. And Tom was reluctant to throw any more money our way, especially as it looked like Windhollow's second album was going to be delayed, if it was recorded at all.

So there was a lot of tension about that, too. There was tension about everything. Those last few weeks at Wylding Hall were pretty miserable, all around.

The weather came down, too. All summer there'd been no rain: all of a sudden it's cold and pissing rain nonstop. The place was freezing, and water came in everywhere. We started seeing rats and mice and voles running through the halls, flushed out by the rain. It was like a biblical curse.

I finally rang up Tom and said, "I'm done." It wasn't the end of the month yet but I could see nothing was going to happen down there, except maybe we'd kill each other out of frustration and sheer bad vibes. As I recall he didn't argue.

But he didn't offer to drive down and help us pack up, either, or put a cheque in the post. I rang off with him then rang Nancy and said, "Come get me soon as you can". Bless her, she came the next day.

I told the others I'd help them pack whatever they wanted into the van, but after that I was gone. I was done. Done, done, done.

Ashton

Everything fell apart after Julian left, especially when we tried to rehearse. We were all thrown off-balance. As a person, Julian was so quiet, but his guitar moved under and within all we did. It was like a hidden tributary, and we didn't know how much it gave to all of us until he was gone.

Will split first. We were all beginning to get paranoid around each other. Suspicious. There was a sense that any of us might have been to blame for Julian going missing. Did I say something that upset him? Did Lesley, or Jonno, or Will? It never crossed my mind that one of us might have hurt him—I mean, really hurt him. It was the police came up with that mad idea when they questioned Les. They talked to all of us , but they came down hardest on her.

And you can see why. She was the only one of us who might have had a motive to kill him, out of jealousy. A crime of the heart. Mind you, I never thought that, none of us did, except for the Alton police detective.

So Will left, and Les soon after. Will shacked up with Nancy at her flat in Brixton. Lesley didn't have a place to stay, so she moved in with them. Jonno and I stuck around for another week or so. One morning we just looked at each other and said, "Well that's it, then." We packed up whatever was left, which wasn't much, threw it into the van and hit the road. I siphoned some petrol from Julian's Morris Minor and left a note inside, telling him I'd pay him back when I saw him. As far as I know, his car's still there.

Billy

I was back at school after the summer holidays. This would have been end of September. I joined the camera club. It met once a fortnight, and at the first meeting they told everyone to shoot a roll of film, develop it then bring the prints to the next meeting. One or two people had a darkroom, but I didn't, and the school didn't.

My camera was a little Instamatic. It had colour film that came in a cartridge. Very convenient. The photo quality was crap, but what did I know? I went with my mum when she went into Alton to do her shopping, dropped off my film at Boots then picked it up the next weekend.

I was so excited! But the film quality truly was crap. Very bright, super-saturated colours, high contrast. Cheap and cheer-ful. The co-lours were a bit surreal—a sort of psychedelic feeling. The frame size was square, which as it turned out was perfect for an album cover.

You got twenty frames to a roll. They printed out as neat lit-tle squares. If you blew them up they were very, very grainy. But they were snapshots, not professional photos, so no one blew them up.

I looked at the photos right away in the car—my mother was driving. I told you that I didn't know what I was doing with that camera, and there was the proof in front of me. The first ten photos, you couldn't even tell what they were supposed to be of. It looked like I'd been taking pictures inside a cave. All blurred and dark. The ones that weren't dark were so overexposed it looked like a nuclear bomb had gone off, except you could see my thumb in the corner.

So the first ten of the twenty photographs were a dead loss, and I wasn't optimistic about the rest. I hadn't had the presence of mind to buy another roll of film at Boots. I thought I'd be screwed come the next camera club meeting. I turned over the next photo and was so stunned I swore out loud—in front of my mother, which I never did! She looked at me like I'd lost my mind. For a second, I thought maybe I had, too.

Tom

One Saturday afternoon at the end of September, Billy Thomas rings me up at the Larkspur office, so excited he can hardly speak. I had to ask him to slow down, and even then all I could make out was something about a stranger at Wylding Hall. I thought he was ringing because the place had been burgled.

Finally I get it out of him that he'd processed the roll of film he'd taken at Wylding Hall the day I'd brought the mobile unit down. Something had shown up in the photos and he wanted me to see it. He *needed* me to see it—he was thinking of taking the photographs to the police.

"Whoa there!" I said.

Actually, what I said should not be repeated. I'd already begun to have some dealings with the police, after Mr. and Mrs. Blake notified them that Julian was missing. I'd sunk almost every penny I had into Windhollow Faire's summer vacation at Hell Hall, and now I had nothing to show for it but a runaway guitarist and some psychedelic field recordings.

And now there's some yokel telling me he's got photos he wants to take to the police. I thought he was blackmailing me, so I told him I'd take him to the police if he tried to contact me again, and I hung up. He tried ringing back but I told my secretary not to answer. I considered calling my solicitor as a protective measure, in case this kid really did have some incriminating photos.

Next thing I know, the following morning I'm alone at the Moon-thunder office, trying to salvage something from the entire Wind-hollow Faire disaster, and who shows up at the door but Bill-the-lad with an envelope of colour snapshots.

"I'm calling the police," I told him.

"I'm not blackmailing you!" He stuck his foot in the door before I could slam it in his face. "Ask Jonathan, I spoke to him last night!"

At that moment, right on cue, the phone rings. And it's Jonno.

"Listen, Tom," he says, "I have no idea what this kid's been smoking, but he sounds harmless. Probably he just wants a job. Hear him out and look at his photos and send him on his way home. There's a train at noon."

Well, as you know, Jonno has a heart big as the national debt. So I sigh and ring off with him and tell the boy he has five minutes to say his piece, before I throw him out and get back to juggling the books.

"We use professional photographers here for anything having to do with the bands, and graphic designers," I told him. I'd already spoken to Hipgnosis, hoping they could do the album cover art. Since it was seeming like there wouldn't be any album, this was turning into a moot point.

"Just look," he said.

He clears off a desk and lays out ten photos like a deck of tarot cards; very, very carefully, like he's putting them in a special order. When he's finished, he points to me and says, "Look."

They were the pictures he'd taken in the garden at Wylding Hall. Informal photos—everyone at their mike stands, singing or playing in the sunlight. A few photos of them messing around, tossing roses at each other.

The last three just showed them all looking up at the sky. Ashton was to the left of the frame. Jonno stood in front of his drum kit. Will and Les were side by side, both shading their eyes. Julian was slightly off by himself to the right, neck craned as he stared up.

The light was clearly different in these pictures—very bright, low-slanting sunlight. It made the grass look golden, and all the other colours stand out more brightly. They weren't terrible photos, but they weren't anything approaching professional quality. Just amateur snapshots.

I turned to the boy and said, "Yes, these are very nice. But as I told you, we—"

"You have to look at them. These three." He indicated the photos where everyone stared at the sky. "Tell me what you see."

It was a minute before I saw it. Inside the walled garden with the others was a sixth person. While the band were all looking at the sky, someone else stood to the right and gazed straight ahead, into the camera. In the first picture the figure was perhaps twenty feet from Julian. In the next photo, it was closer. In the last of the three, it stood directly behind him, and I could see it was a girl, wearing a sleeveless white dress.

"What the hell is this?" I looked at Billy Thomas.

"You tell me."

I glanced at the photos again—all of them, in order. I shook my head. "Did you doctor these? Is this some kind of joke?"

"I swear to you on the Holy Bible, this is how they came out."

I stood and stared at the pictures. I tried to recall everything I could about that afternoon. I'd been inside the mobile unit, but the back doors of the lorry had been open the whole time, so I could watch whatever was going on as I worked the boards. I hadn't moved from there except once, to take a piss.

I remembered exactly when these photos had been taken—I'd yelled at Billy not to trip on the cables as he scampered around. I remembered the sunlight, which had been so beautiful that day. There were only ten shots, so it can't have taken him more than twenty or thirty minutes, if that.

And there had been no one at Wylding Hall that afternoon, except for the members of the band, and Billy, and me.

I looked over at Billy. "That afternoon, when you took these—did you see anyone?"

He shook his head. "There was no one."

"Pick those up and follow me," I ordered him. "Back here."

Moonthunder's art department was a storeroom where we had a mimeograph machine, some light boxes, a filing cabinet and a table covered with photos, design sheets and layouts for album art. I swept these aside, pointed to where Billy should put the photos, and found a loupe and a magnifying lens. I kept the loupe, gave him the magnifying glass, and turned on the table lamp, which was very bright. We couldn't afford a proper light table, but these pictures were so small it would hardly have made much difference.

I spent the next hour scrutinising those photos—the only reason I stopped was that I could feel a migraine coming on. With the loupe, it was crystal clear that the person was indeed a teenage girl, fourteen or fifteen or sixteen. Billy's age. There was nothing fuzzy about her image—it wasn't in any way blurred or hazy or transparent. She looked as solid and real to life as everyone else.

"Do you know her?" I glanced at Billy. "From school, or the pub? Is she a relative of yours?"

"A relative?" He laughed. "No girl in my family would be allowed to run around like that. Besides, all my cousins live in Farnham."

"And you don't recognise her from school?"

"It's a small school. I've known everyone since we were kids." He hesitated, then said, "She looks like the girl they talked about. The one from The Wren. The girl who went off with Julian Blake."

I felt like my head was going to explode. "This is crazy. Some-one must have doctored these. Or, I don't know, swapped them out for some other photos. Where'd you get them developed?"

"Boots. I already called them. They send it out for processing to a place where they have a machine that they run the film through. It's all done automatically. The only thing a person does is stick them in the envelope and hand it to you. And take your money."

We stared at each other across the table and for a long time said nothing. Billy was the one who finally spoke.

"Do you think I should bring them to the police?"

"Why the hell would you do that?"

"Because it might help them find him. And her—both of them."

I thought about that, then said, "No. There'd be too many questions. None of which we could answer," I added, gazing at the pictures. "Look, can I keep these? Just overnight? I promise I won't do anything to them—I won't destroy them or anything like that."

Billy nodded. "Yeah, sure. I have the negatives at home."

"Smart lad. You have my word. Any objection to me blowing these up? Enlarging them so I can look at them more closely?"

"I guess not."

He looked a little put out, so I said, "How's this—if I can make use of these, I'll pay you a professional's fee, and give you photo credit. If I can't make use of them, you let me keep these and give me the negatives, and I'll pay you a hundred pounds."

His eyes got big, but he made a show of thinking it over before he nodded. "Okay."

We shook on it and I told him I'd ring him up after I'd had a chance to look over the enlargements. I thought I'd flatter him by suggesting he'd be a pro—I had no intention of doing anything with those photos, except destroy them.

Jon

Tom called me, demanding to know what the hell was going on with Billy Thomas and these photos. As I hadn't seen the photos, I told him I had no effing clue. Billy hadn't told me anything about them, other than the fact they weren't what he'd expected and he thought someone from the group should see them. I was the only one whose telephone number he had. I didn't want to be bothered, so I told him to ring Tom. After leaving Wylding Hall, I'd had to move back in with my parents in Muswell Hill, and I wasn't too happy about anything right then.

About a week later Tom rings me up again and tells me to come by the Larkspur offices next morning. He wanted to see everyone, he said. It was very important.

Uh oh, I thought.

Lesley

We all went over to Tom's office. Me and Will went together, so at least we had moral support. I'd spoken to Ashton and Jonno on the phone after they'd gotten the call. I assumed Tom was going to sack us—cancel our contract and tell us we were on our own. We'd still have the first album and whatever piddling royalties that generated, after he'd been paid back for everything he'd spent on Wylding Hall. Without Julian, we no longer had a second album, or a band. Windhollow Faire was dead.

Ashton

Tom waited till we all arrived, then led us into the back room, where the photos were all laid out on a table. He didn't say anything except, "Look," and stood back to wait for our reactions.

I thought it was some elaborate, incredibly cruel joke he was pulling. I think everyone else felt the same, except for Les. She actually had to run out of the room because she got sick. By the time she returned, Will and I were shouting at Tom, and Les and Jonno had to pull us off before we knocked him down.

Jon

I knew immediately that they weren't fakes. They were very grainy, more like cheap newsprint photos, but they were real. What else could they have been? It looked just like her, the girl who'd run off with Julian.

Only the photos had been taken a week before that happened. And, of course, she hadn't been there the day we did the outdoors recording.

Tom

It took me a good quarter of an hour to get them all calmed down. I explained as best I could about the photos—which wasn't much explaining at all, just sharing of information. I'd bought loupes for them all, so everyone spent an hour looking through those pictures like they were searching for gold dust. They were 8x10 enlargements, cropped to accommodate the square format of the film. Like I said, not the best quality, but it was clear to me that they weren't fakes.

When everyone else appeared to have accepted that much, they all stopped arguing and looked at me.

Lesley said, "Now what?"

We debated it all afternoon, into the night and the following morning. At one point we broke for dinner, Jonno ran out for take-away and Will popped down to the Off License and bought some whiskey.

The consensus we finally came to was that the three photographs were real. The figure staring out at us was the same girl everyone had seen at the pub a week later. It appeared that she had stepped out from the woods behind the walled garden, and that her intent was to reach Julian. Why she was staring directly into the camera was anybody's guess.

Who she was—*what* she was—was another matter entirely. We never figured that one out. Everyone had a different theory. Mine was that everything that had occurred—up to and including our arguments around the table in the Moonthunder office—was a horrible group hallucination. Sadly, this didn't seem to be the case.

Ashton

The photos were truly frightening. Not the first group, where we're all playing around in the grass, throwing roses at each other and laughing. I love those pictures. I think they capture what was best about Windhollow Faire, what was best about all of us. That was our golden moment—we were all young and beautiful and gifted, and so incredibly fortunate to have found each other. That was the peak. It was pure serendipity that Billy Thomas was there with a camera to capture it.

The other photographs...I hardly like to *think* about them, let alone talk about them. When we had the vote as to whether it should be the album cover, I was the one who voted no.

I know that seems out of character. I'm the one who always laughed or lost my temper when anyone would start to go on about the occult. I believe that there is a rational, scientific explanation for everything. But I have never been able to understand or explain those photographs.

So I voted no. I would not be swayed. We all agreed that the other two photos should remain unpublished. Technically Billy owns them, but he agreed that he wouldn't ever make them available to the public. Especially now, when they could go viral in a heartbeat. He's a man of his word and I trust him. He never had a career as a photographer—he became an estate agent back in the village, as you know. So it's not like these are lost photographs that would revive his career. Or ours.

There were three pictures in which you could see her. The first one, she's at the back of the garden towards the woods, on the right-hand side of the frame, same as Julian, who was staring up at the sky along with the rest of us.

You might almost think she's a statue. She's facing the camera directly, hands at her sides, bare-legged, wearing the same white dress as when I first saw her. Too far off to get a proper look at her face. There was a bit of a breeze, you can see the grasses rippling and everyone's long hair blown by the breeze. Her hair, it hung lank and straight to her shoulders, unmussed by the wind, and the dress straight to her knees. That's the photo on the album cover.

The second one, she looks exactly the same. Only now she's about fifteen feet closer to the camera, maybe ten feet behind Julian; who does not appear to have moved a fraction of an inch. None of us have. We're all in the exact same positions as the previous photo, all still gazing at the sky.

The only way you'd even realise any time has passed is if you look really carefully. You can see Julian's hair has been blown across his cheek, and Lesley's eyes are closed—she blinked. The light is near-ly unchanged, a few more tiny shadows thrown across the grass as that flock of birds flew in front of the sun. I'm still shading my eyes, staring along with the rest. It's very clear that Billy took that photo immediately after the first one, a millisecond later.

So how did the girl move so quickly across the lawn? It's like she's a chess piece someone slid across the grass in a straight line. You can see her better in this one. Her white dress was soiled at the hem, her hands are clenched into fists. You can see her face. Her eyes are open and you can see there's hardly any iris in them at all. They're black and staring right at you without any expression. Her mouth is open. Not all the way open but her lip curled back so you can see a bit of her front teeth. Like a dog starting to snarl.

In the final picture she's right behind Julian, still moving in that unbroken line across the grass; a bit to the side so you can see her clearly, perhaps a foot away from him. He doesn't see her. None of us see her. We're all still gazing up at the sun.

But now she's so close you can see that her eyes are utterly black. No iris, no pupil, no sclera. There might be something in there but I don't want to think what it might be. Just these round black holes. Her skin is so white the capillaries look like a web covering her face. Her hands are turned outwards and her fingers have started to un-clench, white fingers with sharp little nails. Her mouth gapes open as though she's screaming. And you can see that inside it she has more than one row of teeth.

Lesley

It was too ghastly for words. I was sick to my stomach, first time I saw them. They all stayed in there arguing, as though that might explain anything. I could hear them from across the hall and that was bad enough. Just knowing those photos existed was bad enough. The only reason I went back inside was because Will finally came to check if I was all right. He said we all needed to decide together: What were we going to do with the pictures?

Tom

We put it to a vote. Ashton voted no. The others all said yes. And me, of course. It was only after we voted to use it as the cover art for the album that Jon asked, "*What* album?"

I don't know, it sounds mad but I'm a bit mad. You had to be, to be successful in the music business. But all at once it came to me that we should release the tapes we'd recorded in the garden that day. No one had ever done such a thing—Dylan wouldn't release his basement tapes for three years. To release an album of songs that were essentially demos sounded like career suicide for a band that had only released one studio album, from a smallish record company like Moonthunder.

Les asked, "What about Julian?"

"What about Julian? Sod Julian!" I shouted. I was starting to get stroppy. We were all exhausted, half-drunk, hoarse from arguing, and scared out of our wits.

And I had a very strong feeling that Julian was not going to be coming back. Call it a premonition, call it common sense, call it a perfectly reasonable reaction to those three photos—call it whatever you like, but I thought he was gone for good. Gone for the foreseeable future, anyway.

I'd been talking up Windhollow Faire's follow-up album for months. I'd paid for advertising, scheduled studio time, contacted session musicians. If the album didn't appear in the next few months—if we waited for Julian to return before doing a proper studio take—we would miss our chance to cash in on Christmas sales. I was broke. The band were broke.

But I had heard those rough tapes—I was the only one who had. And while the sound quality was iffy in places, overall the songs held up well.

Better than that—if you discounted the sound of bees and wind in the grass and Billy laughing in the background and the in-between-songs chatter, the performances were brilliant. The song writing by Julian and Les was superb, and the covers were well-chosen. Only nine songs all told, but enough to fill up two sides of vinyl.

I knew that if I couldn't convince the band right then and there, the chance would be lost. They'd go their separate ways, which is pretty much what they did end up doing, and I'd be left with nine beautiful songs that no one would ever hear.

Tom

Tom talked us into releasing the live recordings from Wylding Hall. Actually, he held us hostage—he wouldn't let us leave the office until he played them for us.

He was right: they were pretty brilliant. We listened to the tapes twice, all the way through each time. After the freak-out over Billy's photos they were a breath of fresh air. We'd all been up for twenty-four hours by then—not for the first time, but it was a very emotional experience.

Imagine if you could go back and repeat one of the best days of your life—that's what it was like. Lesley cried, hearing Julian sing, but we still assumed he'd be back. At least I did. So we took a vote and everyone voted yes. And then we all went home.

Everyone was completely knackered. Lesley couldn't keep her eyes open and I was walking into walls. Tom saw us out; he promised he'd talk to Billy and sort everything with the photos and get contracts to us as soon as possible.

And so he did. Six weeks later, twenty-fifth of November, *Wylding Hall* was released; the feast of St. Catherine, she of the Catherine Wheel—which is a type of firework, and also a torture device. Which seemed appropriate.

NEW MUSICAL EXPRESS, DECEMBER 1972
Short Reviews: Windhollow Faire, "Wylding Hall"
Review by Patricia Kenyon

LONDON-BASED FOLK OUTFIT *Windhollow Faire upsets the*
trad applecart with Wylding Hall, *follow-on to their epony-*
mous debut album. Wylding Hall *expands the boundaries of*
psychedelic folk far, far beyond the likes of Strawbs, Fairport
Convention and even the Incredible String Band. With their
new record, Windhollow doesn't open the sonic doors of per-
ception so much as blast them apart with a deceptively bucolic
plein air album, courtesy of maverick studio Moonthunder
Records. From the album opener, Lesley Stansall's exquisite
"Cloud Prince", on through Julian Blake's eerie closer, "Thrice
Tosse These Oaken Ashes", the album more than delivers on
the band's promise. One for the ages.

Patricia Kenyon

What a beautiful album that was: like a midsummer day in the
middle of winter. All the reviews were strong. *NME* ran my piece on
the band the same week the disc was released, along with my review
of *Wylding Hall.* They got a nice little boost from that.

The cover helped—that striking photograph of everyone staring at the sky with that unearthly light, like they were watching an atomic blast.

And the girl in white—everyone was talking about the girl. Who she was, what she symbolised.

I recognised her the instant I saw the cover. She was the same girl I'd seen in the library at Wylding Hall when I was there that summer. But I had no more idea than anyone else as to who she was.

Back then people pored over album covers like they were tea leaves or tarot cards. What does Led Zeppelin's fourth album mean? What's it even called?

Everyone had a theory about the cover of *Wylding Hall*. By then, everyone knew that Julian Blake had gone walkabout, and somehow people linked that with the white girl. I certainly did. I tried calling Les and Jonno and the rest, to ask them about it, but they wouldn't return my phone calls. Tom Haring just laughed at me.

"It's a mystery, darling. Why would I solve it and spoil the fun?"

He meant spoil the album's sales. People were buying it as a Christmas gift—I gave copies to my two brothers, and I knew some folks who found duplicates under the tree. It was definitely on heavy rotation on Radio Three during the Christmas hols.

The only thing the band didn't get out of it was a hit single. Sometimes you get a hit right away. Just as often, it takes a few months for word of mouth and airplay to build interest.

Also, you need to perform, and Windhollow Faire didn't do that. I'm not sure why. Julian Blake was an integral part of the group, no doubt about that, but they could have found someone to fill in for him. Richard Thompson, Roy Harper. Even just the four remaining members could have done something.

And the album never got enough airplay. Radio Three and Radio Caroline played it, but it never broke into the big commercial stations. After a few months, it all sort of disappeared. Led Zeppelin's *Houses of the Holy* came out and everyone was talking about that—had they produced another "Stairway to Heaven"? We all had to buy the new Zeppelin album to decide.

In the meantime, *Wylding Hall* lost momentum and never regained it. The album got buried and, within a few years, mostly forgotten.

Ashton

Tastes change. First glam rock was big, then punk. There was still an audience for acid folk, but it got squeezed by the next big thing, whatever that turned out to be. We'd never been in the folkie mainstream long enough to build up much of an audience there. I begged the others to play a few gigs with me, but they refused. Everyone has their reasons, I understand that, but they tossed that album under a bus.

In the long run, that worked in our favour. A few years ago, when Devendra Barnhart, Mumford and Sons, and Roxanna Starkey began talking it up, vinyl copies were going for a hundred pounds—if you could find one. Our record had seemed to be everywhere that Christmas, but when we got our royalty statements, it turned out that only a couple of thousand copies were sold. It never went into a second pressing.

But since the 1980s, some people had been passing around bootleg copies on cassettes and CD. Tom Haring jumped all over that. He threatened folks with legal action, then got in touch with a few of the famous people who loved the album and asked them to blog it or tweet about it. He re-mastered the tapes, and released *Wylding Hall* online as a twofer with our first album. A lot of bands started to cover "Windhover Morn" and add our songs to their set list.

That's when we finally began to see real sales, and real money. That's when fans began to come out of the woodwork. That's when the cult of Julian Blake exploded.

Will

Oh yeah—Windhollow Faire, the missing years. None of us actually disappeared, you know, except for Julian. Me and Nancy split up a year after *Wylding Hall*. Les was still living with us in Brixton, and something was bound to happen. I mean, Les was seventeen and at the height of her beauty. Who could resist her?

We all handled it in relatively civilised fashion. Nancy moved out and Les stayed on. After the first year or two, the dust settled. We'd see each other at parties or gigs and it seemed kind of futile to pretend we didn't know each other. Far too much water under the bridge for that. We're closer now than we were then—Nancy is like a sister to me and Les.

It was a bit more sketchy with the others, Ashton in particular. He couldn't forgive us for not performing as Windhollow Faire, especially when Les and I formed Greenleaves and had a hit with "Copredy Carnival". He went on to do a lot of session work, a lot of jazz recordings. Good bassists are scant on the ground. We made it up eventually and we're all good friends now, but there were years we didn't speak to each other.

Jonno struck off on his own and joined the Blazing Hammers. Got back to his rock and roll roots. They've kept him busy ever since, still draw a crowd in some places—they're big in Brazil.

Nance moved to Florida years ago, to a tiny village called Cassadega; a spiritualist community, psychics and witches and what-have-you. Mediums. She makes a good living from it, and I say more power to her. Les and I have visited several times and it's lovely. Palm trees, not too far from Daytona Beach. She does readings online and over the phone, you should check out her website—oakenashes.com

Jonno

Billy and I stayed in touch over the years. He comes up to London whenever the Hammers play, saw us overseas when he was on holiday. He's an estate agent in the village now. It's become a big place for retirees and second homes. He's done quite well. He knows the area like the back of his hand, knows everyone in town.

The photos were just a flash in the pan. He never pursued it, far as I know. It would be an expensive hobby for a farm boy. When Barry and I started looking for a place outside of London we called him up, and ended up getting our house through him. So now we see him and his boyfriend quite often. I was down in the spring, and that's when he told me about the construction at Wylding Hall.

Billy

Wylding Hall has absentee owners now, they live in Dubai. I keep an eye on the place for them. They want to put plumbing in the old wing, but they needed to get permission from the local council before they started tearing up the grounds. Some of the old-timers don't like the idea. I know my granddad wouldn't have approved.

Tom

I worked out a deal with Billy Thomas. I paid him outright for fair use of his photograph on the album cover, a quite decent sum for an amateur. Then I paid him another thousand quid to hand over the negatives and the original prints. He asked me what I was going to do with them. I said I'd keep them, all except for the last two. Those I intended to destroy.

He didn't put up any argument. He'd seen the pictures—for all I knew, he might have known something about that girl. Local knowledge. Whatever his reasons, he had no objection to the terms of our deal. A thousand pounds was a huge amount of money in 1972. I hadn't exactly set him up for life, but the money gave him a stake for whatever he wanted to do after school.

He didn't seem like the uni type, so I suggested he take some of it and travel once he'd graduated. He did—knocked around Europe for a while on a Eurail pass, I think he went down to Tangier at one point. Settled in London for a few years, then decamped back to his hometown and hung out a shingle as an estate agent.

I destroyed the photos—but only the last two. Set them on fire that afternoon in the Moonthunder office, right after the others left. Burned them in the waste bin. A terrible stink they made, too.

There's no chance I'll forget what they looked like. That girl's face is burned into my mind's eye like a hot spark. I could see her clear as yesterday if I closed my eyes and thought about it. But you couldn't pay me enough money to do that, ever.

EAST HAMPSHIRE ECHO
April 14

RENOVATION OF THE OLDEST WING of *Wylding Hall* has been halted as the result of an unanticipated discovery: a Neolithic passage grave beneath the 14th century manor house. A construction crew led by Morris Taggersell of Taggersell Builders came upon the prehistoric structure when they moved a massive eight-ton boulder under a corner foundation.

"I'm accustomed to finding surprising things during site work, but never something like this," Taggersell said yesterday. "The owners have been contacted and they have agreed to suspend any new construction until a proper assessment has been made."

Preliminary examinations by an archeological team from the University of Winchester has turned up flint arrowheads and other weapons, glass and bone beads, and a number of animal skeletons, as well as a human femur and skull. Carbon dating will provide additional information as to exactly how old the site is.

Chief archaeologist Dr. Elise Rossi made an even more surprising discovery when she unearthed a man's modern wristwatch amongst a cache of grave goods that also included stone bird figurines and a bone flute.

"We have absolutely no idea how that got in there," she said. "There's no sign whatsoever of any kind of disturbance that might have caused its inclusion with the grave goods." Dr. Rossi added that carbon dating would not be necessary for that particular artefact.

Nancy

Will forwarded me the article about the construction—Jonno had sent it to all of them. Les was the one most upset about it, she rang me up. We hadn't talked for about a year, so after she vented for a bit we caught up. She sounds good, happy with Will after all these years. Much better match for him than I would have been.

What do I think it all means? I believe there could be any number of explanations, but I don't feel comfortable discussing it.

Ashton

I've told you what I think. Julian is dead. The girl too, probably. Murdered and buried, or their bodies dropped into the sea.

Or drug overdose, or death by exposure from sleeping rough.

Or he might be in a mental institution—he was obviously going off the rails. He might have become so out of it, he forgot who he is. That happens sometimes. So maybe he's in a loony bin somewhere.

But I don't think so. I think he met some horrible fate, and it's a blessing we don't know about it. That's why I don't like talking about it. One reason, anyway.

Will

The photos I saw in the pub—the hunting of the wren—the song Julian unearthed and a half-naked girl with feathers on her feet... it all adds up, doesn't it?

Les

Jonno floated me his idea for us all getting together there in the summer, if Billy can arrange something with the owners. I'm not sure how I feel about that. I'd love to see everyone, I'm just not sure I want to see them all *there*. But I'll wait to hear what the others think. We'll see.

Jonno

I've always felt that if Julian was dead, I would know it. He was such a big person in so many ways, his talent and his beauty, his belief that the world held a mystery he wanted to unlock. If he were actually dead, there would be such an absence in the world. And I don't feel that.

There's something else, too, something I've never told anyone, not even Barry. I would just as soon tell it now, for anyone who wants to know. I'll just hope the others won't hold it against me.

Eight years ago, Barry and I were on holiday in Corfu. There was a festival going on, a saint's day with a big procession and all kinds of celebrating and a massive crowd. Marching bands, street musicians, parades. People carrying ancient effigies and relics. Like that.

I was squeezing through the crowd on my own. Barry hates crowds, so he stayed back at the hotel. I kept my head down to make sure I didn't step on someone or trip. Eventually the street widened and I could look up again. It was still a huge throng, but I could breathe, at least.

And I saw Julian, I saw Julian Blake, edging through the crowd. The girl, too. I was so shocked I couldn't say anything, but then I shouted out his name.

He didn't hear me. Neither of them did. It was so loud, I couldn't hear myself. The girl didn't look at me, and thank God for that.

But Julian did. Julian stared right at me. I started towards him but at that moment an entire children's orchestra came parading through the street. I tried to push my way through but it was too late. He was gone. They both were gone.

Yet it couldn't have been him. Because he looked exactly the same as he did the last time I saw him, over forty years ago. He hadn't aged a day. Neither of them had.

And he didn't know me, even when I was shouting his name over and over again. Just stared through me like I wasn't even there. And then he was gone.

FINIS